Cuban Grit:

A Modern Tale of Revolution

By John Phillips

First Printing: 2015

ISBN <978-1508527480>

For more information please contact:

John Phillips
8000 Atlantic Avenue
Virginia Beach, VA 23451

Table of Contents

Chapter 1

It is Christmas day in Havana, 2024, Javier Hernandez, is enjoying his morning coffee while watching his seven year old son Orlando open his gifts. Orlando's four grandparents are gathered around the Christmas tree, as are Javier's brother Hector, and his two daughters. The only person missing is Orlando's mother, Vanessa. The loss of Vanessa is a burden that Javier carries with him every day, but the weight of her absence is particularly heavy during the holiday season.

After the initial Christmas morning excitement of watching Orlando open his gifts began to fade, Javier poured a drink of Havana Club Rum to numb the pain he experienced due to the loss of Vanessa. By the time the Hernandez family gathered around the dinner table, Javier was much more open with his thoughts. Even though he received everything he wanted for Christmas, Orlando appeared disheartened sitting at the dinner table.

"Papa, where is my mom, all of the other kids at school talk about their mom's, why don't I have a mom?"

"You know, it was not long ago that we would not have been able to celebrate Christmas in Cuba. When your Grandparents were children, and when I was a child we had a very controlling ruler that wanted to take away all the hope that days like Christmas bring people." Javier thinks about Vanessa, and how to answer Orlando's question.

"OK, but what does that have to do with my mom?"

"Orlando," Javier says with a comforting yet direct voice, "You are right, you are at an age where deserve to know about your mom."

With collective unity Orlando's grandparents quickly interrupt Javier, "Javier! This is not the time or the conditions that you should be having this conversation with Orlando."

"I am talking to my Son!" Javier continues, "Orlando, your mother was an amazing woman. I first fell in love with her when I was only 16." At this point the grandparents are all smiling, but with tears in their eyes. Javier looks back at his son, "When you were born in 2017, Cuba was under the rule of a very bad man, and he created a very tough living situation for all Cubans. Your mother and I were only 19 years old when you first came along, and we thought we were invincible. Once you were born, we knew we wanted to create a better life for you any way that we could. Just shy of your first birthday the very bad man that ruled Cuba stepped down from his position, and in order to prevent another bad man from taking control of the country we joined a revolution.

Although we were only twenty years old, your mother and I led many protests to create a democracy in Cuba, and quickly we were known all over Havana as the leaders of the revolution. Once it was discovered that we were the leaders of the revolution we were targeted by the bad men who wanted to maintain an oppressive government. On December 19, 2018 your mother was killed by an unidentified sniper. Her death was the first death of the revolution. It was the death of your mother that led to the United States military intervening to keep another bad man from coming to power and presumably to free the Cuban people for the first time in 60 years. "

Javier knows that the truth is the Cuban people are still not free. Trust between the United States and Cuba grew in 2015 when the United States started to communicate more directly with the Cuban government in what was stated as an effort to help provide a better life for the Cuban people. Based on this trust the people of Cuba felt confident in the involvement of the United States during the revolution in 2019 and with their plan for advancing Cuba beyond the revolution. After the revolution ended in 2019 the United States began what was to be a one year reconstruction period. The original plan delivered in February 2019 by the newly elected President of the United States Thomas Morgan was for Cuba to be rebuilt with support from the US Government to establish a democratic republic on the island nation. In order to maintain order during the reconstruction period the US military led by General Derrick Wallace would have a presence on the island. It was the belief that after one year of rebuilding that the US would assist Cuba in holding elections. Walking through the streets of Havana in 2025 it appears that the opposite is true, and the United States military presence has increased to a point of militant rule.

Chapter 2

Bo Vance is what many people from the south would refer to as a "good ol' boy." He grew up fishing in the summers and hunting in the winters. Bo was a well-known three sport athlete at Fairhope High School located outside of Mobile in lower Alabama, where he lettered in football, baseball, and basketball. From a young age Bo knew he wanted to serve in the Army the way his grandfather did in Operation Desert Storm. When he graduated high school in 2018 Bo declined football scholarship offers to Alabama, Auburn, and LSU to follow his dream and attend West Point.

Even though he would appear to be the perfect All-American boy, Bo has a dark side not many have ever realized. Bo's parents taught him from an early age that minorities were inferior and useless members of society. Bo realized these views were not tolerated at an institution as prestigious as West Point, so he bottled in his feelings on race relations while closely following the stories coming out of Cuba.

When Bo started at West Point in the fall of 2018, the long ruling Communist leader of Cuba stepped down from his position. While the people of Cuba pursued their freedom, Bo read countless stories of the Cubans protesting and revolting against their government. All Bo could think about when reading about the Cuban

Revolution in 2018 was that the United States needed to put the Cubans in their place before their revolution went too far. Bo was pleased when President Morgan held a press conference to announce to the American public that the United States would be establishing a military presence in Cuba in 2019. When Bo graduated from West Point in 2022 he requested to be put on foot patrol on the streets of Havana, so that he could have a direct impact by putting the Cubans in their place.

In 2022 when Bo arrived in Havana, the military presence was slowing growing to the point that Cubans began having concerns. Being a West Point graduate Bo was quickly given a large territory and his own platoon. Bo wanted to make a name for himself so he and his platoon actively pursued any wrongdoing with extreme aggression. There were multiple occasions where Bo used what even his military colleagues considered excessive force for what were considered petty crimes. Bo and his platoon quickly built a reputation in his territory of Havana as "speaking softly and carrying a big stick" and with this reputation they gained the nickname Rough Riders Resurrected.

Bo's reputation drew the attention of Commanding General Wallace. General Wallace was known as a hard ass, and he appreciated the reputation that Bo Vance had earned. With the assistance of General Wallace's recommendations Bo quickly moved up the ranks and in the process took on greater responsibility. In April 2025 General Wallace appointed Bo to the position of his "right hand man" with the formal title of Vice Commander of Military Operations in Cuba. General Wallace decided that Bo would handle all ground operations in Cuba while the General would handle the administrative actions and communicate directly with President Morgan.

Chapter 3

Back in 2018 Javier and Vanessa were leaders of the Cuban Revolution in Havana. They led rallies of thousands in the squares around Havana often narrowly escaping arrest. Cuban citizens did not have the right to peacefully assemble, so hundreds of other Cubans were arrested in these same protests. The hope of Javier, Vanessa, and the thousands of other Cubans that were part of these protests was that even without violence their message would be heard, and fearing a hostile takeover the leaders of Cuba would abandon their Communist rule. When Vanessa was killed on December 19, 2018, the United States took the worldwide outrage over the unnecessary death of a young and vibrant woman as an opportunity to overthrow the Cuban government. In February 2019, after the newly elected President Thomas Morgan took office, the United States sent in 50,000 troops to the streets of Havana to back the revolution.

The people of Cuba were thrilled knowing that with the assistance of their neighbor to the north that Cuba would be forever changed. It was the belief of the nation that they loved would finally be free. Simple rights such as freedom of speech, freedom of religion, and freedom for enterprise would finally be theirs. With their new found optimism, the Cuban people welcomed with United States with open arms. However, the involvement of the United States left more questions than answers for Javier.

"Why did the love of his life or anyone for that matter have to die before the Americans would help? Why did the Americans suddenly care about the people of Cuba? What really were the intentions of this much larger and much more powerful country?" Even with all of his questions Javier was too depressed with the loss of Vanessa to make much of a case to anyone. If he was able to work up the nerve to discuss his thoughts on the United States military occupation in Cuba, his opinion would be dismissed because of his state of mind due to the loss of Vanessa.

On June 26, 2019 the Cuban government collapsed. From that day forward, June 26, 2019 would be known as Dia de La Revolucion Finale (Day of the Final Revolution). The diplomatic agreement between the United States and Cuba was for 5,000 American military troops to remain in Cuba in an effort to maintain peace. More importantly the agreement also stated that the United States would support Cuba as a United States territory, and provide political assistance to Cuba as they transitioned to a democratic republic. The agreement was that once both Cuba and the United States agreed that Cuba could once again function as an independent nation, that the United States would leave Cuba, and allow their democracy to flourish. President Morgan began the path to democracy by establishing the first truly free election in Cuba in over 50 years. The election would be for Governor of Cuba, and the Governor would presumably work with the presidentially appointed Commander of Military Operations in Cuba, General Wallace, to establish the first American controlled government in Cuba. Juan Puig of the newly formed Democratic Republican Party of Cuba won the election.

What did all of this mean for the people of Cuba? Well for one it held promise, it offered hope for a better future, and a chance to provide a better life for their families. Although the people of Cuba wanted Javier to be their first governor, he did not feel the calling to politics. He was burnt out from the revolution, and not in a mental state to lead his people after the death of his beloved Vanessa. Javier had the intelligence, but he did not have the personality. Although he was a natural leader, Javier was much too direct and truthful to be a politician. He did not understand why politicians had to be in the spotlight, and why they were put on such a pedestal. With the admiration he gained from his role in the Cuban Revolution, Javier had his pick of any career he wished. Javier decided that he would take some time to be with his family, raise Orlando, and live a humble life as an announcer for the Havana Knights professional baseball club. Javier hoped he could fade away from the spotlight, but no matter how much time went by Javier remained revered in Havana.

By the first anniversary of Dia de La Revolucion Finale Javier was beginning to develop more optimism towards the changes taking place in his country. Maybe his initial thoughts were wrong; maybe the Americans really did want to help the Cuban people. When the first Dia de La Revolucion Finale Anniversary Celebration took place in Plaza Vieja on June 26, 2020, Javier and his son were the guests of honor. Governor Puig presented Javier and Orlando with a key to Havana, and also with the key to a new house located in a nice neighborhood a short distance away from the city center for his contribution to the Cuban Revolution. Javier did not feel deserving of a new house, but it would have been disrespectful to decline the gracious gift from the Governor. Following the presentation of his new house, Javier gave a compelling speech to the crowd about the future of Cuba, and immediately afterward fireworks erupted. They were the first fireworks that Orlando and even Javier had ever experienced. It looked as though things were finally looking up for Javier and for Cuba.

The trouble with Javier's new found optimism was it blinded him to the truth. Javier would continue to take Orlando to the fireworks every year, but it was not until four years later in 2024 that Javier noticed that with each passing year it appeared that Cuba was not any closer to reaching independence, in fact it appeared as though the US military presence was growing far beyond the agreement of 2019. Javier began to question the gift the Governor Puig had blessed him with. By 2024 it appeared that the Governor's position that was created in 2019 was just one of a figure head to create an illusion of a brighter future. It was clear to Javier that the United States Government was really in control, and that Cuba was just a pawn in their political agenda. Was Javier paid off with a key to Havana and the key to a new house by the United States Government, and he did not even realize it, or was he just being paranoid? Javier grew concerned for the future of Cuba...

Chapter 4

Chevita Alexandra Diaz was born on April 17, 1995 in the University of Miami Hospital as the only child of successful Cuban immigrants, Emmanuel and Isa Diaz. Chevita's parents were teenage sweethearts that through a mixture of love and bravery decided to defect to the United States when they were only sixteen for the chance of a better life. After arriving in Miami in 1980, Emmanuel and Isa moved in with Emmanuel's great uncle Henry to get on their feet. Henry enrolled Emmanuel and Isa in an English course, and following learning English, Emmanuel and Isa earned their General Equivalency Diploma. After receiving their GED, the young couple enrolled in the Miami Dade Community College right on time at age 18. By the time they were 20 they both enrolled at the University of Miami, and pursued degrees in political science and law. When Chevita was born in 1995 Emmanuel was a political science professor at the University of Miami, and Isa was a successful attorney.

Considering the difficult path to success that her parents endured Chevita was born with a silver spoon. While she easily could have just ridden on her parent's coat tails, Emmanuel and Isa made sure to instill their same values in their daughter all the while making sure she knew and respected their story. Chevita was very close with her parents, and even though they were busy with their careers they always made time for her. As their only child, Emmanuel and Isa included Chevita in every aspect of their life, so by the time she was in her teens she was well versed in politics, government, and Miami social scene. When she graduated from high school, she decided to attend her parent's alma mater and double major in political science and communications.

Upon graduation from the University of Miami, Chevita was able to take advantage of the connections she made through her parents to land a job as a news reporter for the local Miami News Channel 13. Chevita was the perfect package for a news reporter, intelligent, focused, personable, and beautiful. In order to appeal to a wider audience Miami News Channel 13 requested Chevita to use a variation of her middle name. Chevita's Miami News Channel 13 name was Alex Diaz. Alex was an excellent reporter, and through the ties she made with her parents she was able to land every big interview. Alex always did her job exactly as she was called to do it, and she quickly became a news anchor at News Channel 13. By the time she was 25 in 2020 she was the face of Miami News Channel 13, and her picture was on billboards throughout the city. Alex's biggest fans were initially the men of Miami who initially tuned in because of Alex's striking beauty. Many of the women of Miami were skeptical at first as they put up with their husbands immature banter about her looks, but over time she grew increasingly popular with the female population of Miami. The women of Miami admired Alex for her intelligence and her position of strength. She was a positive role model for young women throughout Miami, and even at her young age it was clear that she was deserving of her position.

About the time that Alex Diaz was rising to fame with Miami News Channel 13, the hot topic in Miami was the Cuban Revolution. The Hispanic community is very prevalent in Miami, and the majority of the Miami Hispanic community is Cuban-American. Based on the 2010 Census it is estimated that there are one million Cuban-Americans living in Miami. Due to the connection that Miami has with Cuba, Alex was covering the Cuban Revolution nearly every night, including multiple trips to Havana. It was not long before Javier and Vanessa Hernandez were household names in Miami. Alex wondered what it must be like for Javier to lose his wife on that December evening, and now to have to raise a son on his own. Although she had never met Javier, she admired his courage, and the difference he was making in Cuba at such a young age.

Shortly after the United States joined the Cuban Revolution, Alex met her father for dinner at a café in the little Havana neighborhood of Miami Beach. Alex enjoyed having dinner and drinks in little Havana, because although she was famous throughout Miami, she had so much respect within the Cuban-American community that they would give her space to enjoy her downtime. Emmanuel and Alex were enjoying their ropa vieja and mojitos in March 2020, when they first discussed the topic of the Cuban Revolution.

"Chevita, your mother and I watch you on the news every night, and we have noticed how involved you are with the story in Cuba." Said Emmanuel.

"Yes, Papa."

"Well, what are your thoughts on it?"

"I just do my job every day, and try to get the people of Miami the news that matters the most to them."

"Do you have any personal opinion on the Revolution?"

Even in her mid-twenties Alex would often have an attitude with her parents. "I don't know, do we have to talk about work over dinner? I think it makes for a good story, good ratings, and now Americans have a new place to vacation, and better cigars to smoke."

"Chevita, you must care more about it than that! Do you realize what this means? The communist regime is out. The people of Cuba, our relatives, may finally be free. This is huge news not only for Cuba but for society as a whole. It is also important from a political perspective to ask why the United States is truly involved. Right now the media is making it out to be strictly for humanitarian purposes, but I would not be surprised if there is more to it than that. Why is the United States really maintaining a military presence on a Caribbean island ninety miles to our south? Remember to always question the motives of our leaders. You may not realize it, but you are in a position of extreme power, you have the ability to inform and shape the minds of all of your viewers."

"Thanks Papa, but in the big scheme of things I have a relatively small number of viewers, I realize that Miami is a big city, but in comparison with our nation only a very small percentage of our country actually ever hears what I have to say."

"That may be true, but you never know where you may land. You have already rapidly gained local fame, who knows what your future holds."

"I like what I am doing, are you suggesting that I should move to a bigger market?"

"I am suggesting that you use your God given gifts to benefit the world, however you see fit."

"But I would not want to leave you and Mom, and my life in Miami."

"You do not know what life holds for you, but you need to be open to new experiences and follow your dreams. Keep in mind that life is bigger than you, and you should be open to any opportunities where you can make a difference. If your mother and I were not open to new opportunities and willing to take on risks we would still be in Havana, and who knows where we would be in life."

"Thanks Papa, I really appreciate all of your advice, and the life that you and mom have given me."

Chapter 5

On the sixth anniversary of Dia de La Revolucion Finale, Javier took eight year old Orlando to the fireworks at Plaza Vieja. Javier was reluctant to go because of the lack of positive change for Cuba he noticed with every passing year. Being a good father it was too difficult for Javier to tell Orlando that he would not take him to the fireworks because of a reason he knew Orlando would not understand. Orlando was very intelligent for his age, but to him the fireworks were a fun and exciting time that he would be able to spend time with his father and hopefully see some class mates. The square which held the celebration was walking distance from their home. The fireworks were all set to go off at nine, so Javier and Orlando arrived at seven to get a good spot to enjoy the show. Knowing that it would be difficult for Orlando to sit still for two hours, Javier, allowed Orlando to join some of his class mates for a quick baseball game in the park beside the square while he held their spot.

"Papa, can I go over to the park with my friends to play baseball? They need me to be the pitcher."

"Sure Orlando, just be back here as soon as you see the sun start to set. Have fun, and remember the videos I showed you of your second cousin El Duque pitching for the Yankees. Make us proud."

"I will Papa, see you soon."

Javier decided that while he held their spot, he would enjoy his favorite drink of Havana Club and Ginger Ale. Javier was still famous throughout Cuba for his involvement in the Revolution, so while sitting in Plaza Vieja waiting for the fireworks, numerous people came to talk to him and take pictures. Javier did not really understand why he was still famous, but the people of Cuba felt forever indebted to the leader of their latest revolution.

All of the attention Javier was receiving caught the eye of the American soldiers patrolling Plaza Vieja that night. General Wallace made sure to put his best men in Plaza Vieja for the celebration to ensure that the Cubans stayed civil. General Wallace realized that with every passing year without an independent government that the people of Cuba would grow more and more restless, and he suspected that the fireworks on the ground may be more explosive than the fireworks in the sky on Dia de La Revolucion in 2025. In order to stifle any unrest General Wallace assigned his most feared squadron known as the "Rough Riders Resurrected" led by Bo Vance to Plaza Vieja for the celebration. Bo knew that Javier was the leader of the revolution, and Javier still looked exactly the same as he did when he led the revolution seven years prior. Bo kept his eye on Javier waiting to make an example of him, and receive even further notoriety with General Wallace. Bo knew that if he could arrest Javier for any petty offense that the Cuban people would know if their beloved revolutionary leader could be arrested, that any one of them could be as well.

When the sun started to set, Javier began to worry about Orlando. Orlando always listened to his father, so it was concerning to Javier when he did not come back to their spot to watch the fireworks. By the time Javier decided to set out to find Orlando he had already downed several cocktails while socializing and holding his and Orlando's spot. Javier decided that he needed to go find Orlando, so he proceeded to stumble through the square.

When Bo saw Javier stumbling through the square he saw his opportunity. One section of the Diplomatic Agreement of 2019 between Cuba and the United States was to make public intoxication illegal in an effort to better control future crowds. This was a law that had never been enforced in six years, but Bo saw it as an opportunity to make an example out of Javier in an effort to really drive home the point that no one was safe from being arrested under his watch. Bo grabbed Javier, and placed him in handcuffs. Javier remained calm, knowing that his people, the Cuban people, loved him much more than they were afraid of Bo and the "Rough Riders

Resurrected." About this time Orlando saw his father being arrested in the distance, and he panicked.

"Nooooooo! Papa! Don't take him! Don't take my Papa!" screamed the young Orlando.

Orlando's plea was heard throughout the square, and quickly everyone's attention turned to the arrest of Javier. Luckily the sun had not yet set, so the entire ordeal was clearly visible to everyone in the square. Bo underestimated the grittiness of the Cuban people, and the love they have for Javier. Violence quickly erupted in the square. A stone was thrown from the masses which struck Bo on the temple leaving him unconscious. Javier ran to Orlando, and Orlando followed him back to their house where they decided to hide out. The younger Javier would have been right in the center of the disruption in the square, but now his priority was raising Orlando.

Luckily for Javier and Orlando they retreated to the safety of their house, because the tension in Plaza Vieja boiled over into violence. Just as General Wallace feared the only fireworks that erupted that night were on the ground. The Cubans continued to throw stones and fight the American Soldiers until the Soldiers fired tear gas and rubber bullets into the crowd. Rubber bullets are typically non-lethal, but one of the bullets struck eighteen year old Alexis Kuptez in the eye fatally wounding her. Alexis was the first death due to unrest on Cuban soil since the June

26, 2019 Dia de La Revolucion Finale. The crowd dispersed, but the future of Cuba appeared more uncertain than ever.

Chapter 6

June 27, 2025, the day after the Dia de La Revolucion Finale fiasco, and Bo Vance found himself in a hospital bed at St. Christopher Hospital in Havana. He was still feeling dazed and confused when his US Army nurse walked in.

"What happened, where am I?" asked Bo.

"You don't remember? There was an unruly crowd last night at the Dia de La Revolucion Finale celebration, and you were knocked unconscious when a stone thrown from the crowd struck you in the temple. Thankfully your fellow soldiers were able to safely pull you from the crowd and bring you here," responded the nurse.

"Am I going to be ok?"

"You are fine, you just suffered a concussion and a head laceration, but we were able to stich you up without any complications. We just needed to keep you overnight for observation, but you should be able to go home later today."

Bo immediately went from worrying about his health to worrying about the mistake he made in his attempt to arrest Javier. Nothing went the way he suspected. Bo was embarrassed, and he feared the response from General Wallace. Was Javier really as powerful as last night suggested? It appeared as though all the Cubans in Havana stood up for him all at once. Bo really expected the opposite reaction; he really expected that he would instill fear in the hearts of the Cuban people. Bo finally realized he underestimated Javier, and the Cuban people. About the time Bo was finally coming to terms with the outcome of the night before, General Wallace walked into his hospital room.

"How are you feeling," asked General Wallace.

"Fine, Sir," responded Bo.

"You shouldn't feel fine. You really screwed up last night. What were you thinking?"

There was a time when Bo felt as though he and General Wallace were peers. It felt to Bo as if he had taken a step back, and now there relationship changed to one of angry parent scolding a troublesome child.

"I was really hoping to make an example of Javier Hernandez in order to instill fear into the Cuban people. I figured if the people saw Javier get arrested they would know that no one was protected as long as we are in charge. Do you realize who he is?"

"Of course I know who he is. *Do you realize who Javier Hernandez is?* He is the most powerful man in Cuba; he has the backing of all of his people. He likely did not realize his power until your screw up last night showed him exactly what he is capable of. Not only that but you endangered his eight year old son, his anger is surely boiling over. Javier has been quite for years since the revolution, but I'm afraid you may have awoken a sleeping giant. I do not care if your pride is hurt, you are to leave him be, we cannot risk another Cuban Revolution."

"Yes Sir."

Bo realized how costly his mistake may be, but he vowed to himself that he would make up for his mistake. He also realized that his relationship with General Wallace may never be the same, but he would need to put the past behind him to focus on the future.

Chapter 7

On a sunny March afternoon Alex sat on her apartment balcony in South Beach thinking of the dinner she had the week prior in little Havana with her father. She felt that the conversation with her father left her with more questions than answers. Most of the conversations she had with her father went in a similar way, but Alex chalked it up to his experience as a professor. Professor Diaz was always challenging his students to formulate their own thoughts, and she realized in a way she was his most prized student. She considered herself blessed to have a father that challenged her in such a way that made her into a better person.

Alex thought more about what her father said about Cuba and he was right. There is a lot more to the Cuban Revolution than a new place for Americans to vacation, and better cigars for them to smoke. She was embarrassed she had even said that, and relieved that it was only her father who heard it. She thought about how her parents risked everything at the chance of a better life in the United States, and about what a life of despair they must have been experiencing in Cuba in order to take that risk. When it comes down to it, it really is a human rights issue, and that should explain why the United States military was still occupying Cuba. President Morgan must be concerned that if the military leaves too quickly that

Cuba would fall back into a communist government with ties to enemies of the United States. If it were a human rights issue, why would it take so long for the United States to act? Was an embargo truly expected to produce change, or was it really just a passive aggressive way of saying, "Shame on you Cuba we will not support your communist government." The United States has a history of fighting wars in countries thousands of miles away in the name of human rights, so why has it taken so long to do anything about a communist neighbor only 90 miles to our south? There have long been rumors that many of the wars the United States have fought in the Middle East were really over economic concerns particularly surrounding oil. If that were the case, Cuba does not have any natural resources for the United States to profit from, so what would be the reason for us to suddenly be concerned with Cuba? Was her Dad really onto something bigger?

Alex thought more about what her Father suggested for her career. She realized that since she joined Miami News Channel 13 that she has been a pawn to their agenda. She has never really stood up to her executives for her beliefs. Alex always did the stories she was told, without asking any questions. Miami News Channel 13 made her go by a different name. Sure Che was a controversial figure, as he was a hero to some and a villain to others, but that should not mean that she could not use her birth name on the air. Her father also made a good point about the influence she could have with her viewers, she was really much more powerful than she had ever realized. Maybe it was selfish to stay in her comfortable Miami bubble? Maybe she should try to branch out if the opportunity arose. Chevita thought wherever she could reach the most viewers and have the biggest impact is where she belongs.

Alex continued to report the news at Miami News Channel 13 over the next few years. The situation in Cuba quieted down, and although the United States still maintained a military presence on the island, it was no longer a hot topic item. On most nights Alex would report the typical news stories on gang violence, local political corruption, and the increasing cost of living in her city. On occasion she would have the opportunity to report a feel good story about an increase in the manatee population or on a Miami Dolphins victory, but for the most part she lost excitement for her job. She did not realize how blessed she was at the beginning of her career to be on the front line for such a high profile story as the Cuban Revolution. Through it all Alex maintained her popularity in Miami, and continued to gain respect from within the industry.

In February 2025, John Wilson, the CEO of the National News Corporation (NNC) based out of Washington DC was vacationing at his beach house in the

Florida Keys when he caught the Miami news one night. NNC was the parent company for Miami News Channel 13, so he always liked to check in on the local news companies under his cognizance when he was on vacation. He was immediately intrigued by the beautiful young anchor Alex Diaz, so he made a call down to the Miami affiliate for more information on her. After doing his research and listening to Alex's executive producer go on and on about how great she was, John knew he had found his new field reporter to cover the 2026 Presidential election in Washington DC. Between her experience as a news reporter and her degree in political science she was the perfect fit. The CEO side of John Wilson realized that she would have an immediate ratings impact by her looks alone, and that once the nation realized her intelligence she would gain the respect of the nation just as she had in Miami years ago. The trick was just getting her to leave her job as a news anchor in sunny Miami for a job as a field reporter in the often cold and dreary nation's capital.

In May 2025 Alex received a call from CEO John Wilson who offered her a substantial raise to take a position as the primary field reporter for the nightly news broadcasted nationwide every night at six-thirty. The CEO informed her that she would cover the federal level political scene in Washington DC with her primary focus being on the 2026 Presidential election. Alex politely asked the CEO if she could take a night to think about it, and get back to him. Alex would never forget, John Wilson's response, "I have no problem with giving you a night to think about it, as I know this is a big decision. I want you to realize that the opportunity being presented to you is one of those life-changing moments; you will be at the forefront of every political decision in Washington with the opportunity to inform the entire country on a nightly basis. When these life moments are presented you must seize the opportunity, or have a worthy justification that will prevent you from regretting your inaction for the rest of your life. I know that Miami is a beautiful place, but I sure hope for your sake that a little bad weather is not your justification to pass up the opportunity to make a difference in the world here in Washington DC. Have a good night and I will talk to you tomorrow."

Chapter 8

Javier woke up in a haze the morning after the uprising in Plaza Vieja during the Dia de La Revolucion Finale celebration. His hangover from the combination of rum and stress left him with a pounding headache, and he was having trouble putting all the pieces together. Javier wondered how he went into the night with the best of intentions to take his son to see the fireworks, but left with he and his son running back to his house narrowly escaping a violent mob of people. When his son came into his room he looked distraught. Javier was just as upset with how the night concluded, but he wanted to help Orlando relax.

"What's wrong buddy?" Javier asked Orlando with a smile.

"Last night was really scary Dad," Orlando nervously replied.

"It's ok Orlando. I would never let anything happen to you."

"I know Dad, but the soldiers were really angry with you, and they tried to take you away from me, and then everyone there was mad at each other and throwing rocks. I saw blood, and heard people screaming, and I didn't know what to do, so we just ran."

"It's ok, it's ok, we are safe now, do not worry it is all over."

"Thanks Papa, I love you."

Javier seemed to have comforted Orlando, but now he had to make peace with the situation in his own mind. He was shocked at the amount of support the crowd had given him when he was nearly arrested last night. He was even more surprised by the frustration of the Cuban people towards the American soldier's that boiled over from the crowd. Before last night, Javier thought he was alone in his concerns with the continuing United States military presence, and the lack of change to establish an independent Cuban government. After last night it was clear that now was the time to act, something would need to be done to create change, because the status quo would no longer be acceptable. The more he thought about the events of the previous night, the angrier Javier became. "They tried to take me from my son. Why are they even still here? This is supposed to be our Cuba. We fought for our freedom. Vanessa died for our freedom. Our son is still growing up in an oppressive Cuba, only now there is a new oppressor" Javier stewed over his thoughts. Javier decided that he had to do something, so he decided to organize a group of protestors that would shine a light on the United states military presence in Cuba through non-violent means.

On June 28, 2025, a group of twelve men led by Javier met in his basement to discuss the best path forward to a brighter future for Cuba. Javier presented his plan for non-violent protests, but initially not everyone was on board with Javier's plan.

"I think the best plan moving forward would be to lead a series of non-violent protests in all of the main squares of Havana to drum up support throughout the Cuban community. Once we have the support of the community, we will make a bold statement to really drive home the point to the international community." Javier did not see resounding acceptance from the group.

"I think the best plan is to use the weapons given to us by the United States during the Cuban Revolution against them. That would really make a statement," proclaimed Javier's brother Hector.

"Yeah, we are sick of the American soldiers controlling our lives," the group seemed to like Hector's plan better than Javier's.

"What is wrong with all of you? The American's got us to this point. We do not want to hurt them. We just want our freedom. If we try to go up against the American military with violence, we will either be killed or jailed, and likely will never see our families again. Is that what you want? Of course not, besides history has taught us that non-violent protest resonates well with the American public. Look back at the American civil rights movement, Malcom X, believed in "by any means necessary," but Dr. Martin Luther King, Jr. led non-violent protests, which by and large won the respect of both politicians and the American public, resulting in change. Now there is even an American holiday named after Dr. King, and his name will go down in history as having one of the greatest impacts on society ever seen. Would you rather be Malcom X, or would you rather be Martin Luther King?"

"Martin Luther King, was assassinated!" the group yelled at Javier.

"That may be true, but he changed the world. The ignorant sin of one man should not stop you from following his model of change. Let's try it my way first. This may not be an easy process, but we have made change happen before, and we can make it happen again if you trust me. We have all made it through a large amount of adversity, but it is in our Cuban blood to not give up the fight. We must have the strength to face what feels like an endless amount of resistance and still move forward. If you trust me we can change the world."

"Only because you have earned our respect will we try it your way first, but if this continues for too long without any action, we may have to change our course," Hector spoke for the group.

"Glad to hear it. Now that you are all on board, I need you to lead the charge. I will help instruct you on the proper way to conduct these protests, but I must stay out of the public eye for now. I am far too known by both the Cubans and the Americans from the Cuban Revolution, to be seen protesting until the time is right. We want exposure, but we want support first. After we have the support of the people, I will drop the hammer that exposes the American military presence and the frustration of the Cuban people to the world."

After their discussion, the twelve men began to plan a crusade to refocus media attention on the United States military presence in Cuba. Javier preached that they would lead non-violent protests against the US military in Cuba. For too long the US military had been trying to control their lives, and it was time to make a stand. The plan would be to regain international attention through non-violent protests in order to gain the support of the American public to call for an end of the US military occupation in Cuba. Javier was appreciative of what the United States had done for their cause during the Cuban Revolution, but enough was enough, it was time for them to leave. It appeared as though the rest of the world had forgotten the US military still occupied Cuba except for the people of Cuba. Through their non-violent means of protest they would regain international attention, and promote change, with the goal being to create a free and fully independent Cuba.

Chapter 9

Immediately after getting off the phone with John Wilson, Alex thought back to her conversation with her father from nearly five years prior. Alex was not much for spontaneity, but now was her moment. The CEO of a major national news empire had offered her a position, and expected an answer within twenty four hours. Alex did not get more than a couple of hours sleep the night after John Wilson's call. She could not stop the gears from turning in her mind with all the questions she had about her future. She knew she had to call her father. No matter how busy his life, Professor Diaz was always there for his only daughter, and he always knew how to make sense of a difficult decision.

Alex picked up her phone at 7:45 in the morning to call her Dad, "Good morning Papa."

"Good morning Chevita, what an unexpected surprise, I'm not used to hearing from you at this hour of the morning."

"Do you have time to talk?"

Professor Diaz was on his way to his 8:00 am lecture, but would always make time to speak to his daughter, "Sure, is everything ok? You sound tired, and I can hear the stress in your voice." Professor Diaz knew his daughter better than anyone, and was concerned with where this conversation was heading.

"I received a new job offer last night. The CEO of NNC called and offered me a position as his lead field reporter in Washington DC, with my primary job being to cover the 2026 Presidential election. I'm unsure of what to do."

"Congratulations, this is terrific news. I'm confused, why you are so stressed about this decision? What are your concerns?"

"Thanks Papa, I don't know, it just came out of the blue, and I have to give him an answer by tonight. I really do not see myself living in Washington DC, but it is a good opportunity. Also in some ways losing my position as a news anchor to work as a field reporter again feels like a demotion, but I would be able to reach so many more people by working for a national news agency."

"Change is a big part of life, and the ones who are the most successful are the ones who are willing to accommodate for change. You have reached your full potential in Miami; if you stay here you will always be a news anchor for the local news, which is quite an accomplishment in itself. You just need to answer for yourself if you will be happy staying in your current position, or if you see a different future for yourself. Only you can answer that question, and I know you will make the correct decision. One more thing, remember you are in the driver's seat, this man came to you, not the other way around. If you decide to take this job, think about what you really want from the change, and use your position of power to negotiate with him before you accept the position."

"Thanks Papa, I think I have to accept the job. I really appreciate all of the advice. I love you."

"I think that is the right decision, your mother and I will miss having you in the same city, but we will come to visit, and I'm sure you will want to come home to visit too. I love you, Chevita."

Professor Diaz arrived to his class ten minutes late with a proud smile on his face. He then proceeded to tell the class all about his daughter's new position, but his class was not nearly as enthused for his 8:00 am lecture.

Alex was tired of overly thinking about this decision. She had decided that it was time for her to call John Wilson and accept the position. Alex nervously picked up the phone knowing her life was about to change forever.

"Good morning, Mr. Wilson."

"Good morning, Alex, please call me John, hopefully you are calling me with good news."

"I want to let you know that I really took to heart our conversation last night about seizing opportunities when they are presented. I analyzed every aspect of this decision, and what it would mean for my life. I think your offer gives me the greatest opportunity to make a difference in the world, but I have a few demands before I accept the position."

John Wilson was taken back. It was not often that anyone was that direct with the CEO, but he appreciated Alex's directness and was eager to hear what she had to say, "go for it, I'm ready to hear what you have to say."

"I want to start by saying I care more about making a difference in the world than I do any amount of money or fame I can make from this move. I want to have equal power with the executive producers to pick and choose the stories to report on. If I do not think it is important to my viewers, unless a case is made to me why it is necessary, I will not report on it. I want to ensure I have a segment of at least three minutes of air time every night from my start date through the election. Part of this move for me is recreating my identity as a news reporter, and for that reason I want to be able to use my birth name Chevita Diaz when covering the news. Alex is dead."

"Wow, I have to admit I am impressed, I have never had someone I have offered a position put that level of thought into the decision. If I grant you all of these demands are you saying you will come to work for me?"

"Yes, I think this would result in a mutually beneficial arrangement, and a better news broadcast for the viewer."

"Done, you start November 3, 2025 that gives you exactly one year to inform the American public of the upcoming presidential election on November 3, 2026."

"Thank you John, I'm excited to come work for you."

Chapter 10

After dedicating her life to her career for the past five years, Chevita realized she had never taken any time for herself. In fact she had not even taken a vacation since a wild Spring Break in Cancun when she was 21. After her conversation with John in late December, she realized that she had a prime opportunity to take some time for herself, so she immediately put in her two weeks notice with her last day being June 12, 2025. Chevita had accumulated a very large savings, so money was not an issue. This time off was going to be exactly what she needed to gear up for the next stage of her life. As usual Chevita had it all planned out. She would start her time off by spending quality time with her parents with a summer family vacation to southern California. After her family vacation, she would spend a month in Washington DC to find an apartment, meet her new colleagues, and get all of her ducks in a row for her new life. Chevita would then take a much needed personal two week vacation in October at a beach resort in the Caribbean. After relaxing on the beach for two weeks she would come back home to spend the last couple of weeks with her parents and close friends in Miami before moving to Washington DC.

Chevita was really excited about spending time with her parents before her big move, but the part of her break she was most excited about was her two week beach vacation. She did some research to find out the most relaxing place to vacation, and surprisingly she discovered that the nicest all inclusive Caribbean beach resorts were in Cuba. Europeans and Canadians had been vacationing in Cuba for decades, but it was not until 2020 that the United States allowed for Americans to vacation in Cuba. Chevita had a bond with Cuba from her Cuban heritage, and her first news stories after college largely being based out of Havana. It sounded like a natural fit, so she booked her two weeks all inclusive vacation at the Marbella Beach Resort located forty-five minutes outside of Havana. Although she would be traveling by herself, she could not have been more excited about her first vacation in years. This vacation would be the opposite of that crazy week in Cancun for Spring Break in 2018. This week would be about relaxing and rejuvenating before starting her new career in DC.

Chevita arrived in Havana on a beautiful 90 degree day on Monday, October 6, 2025. Although she was fascinated with the changes that must have taken place since her last trip to Havana five years ago, this trip was all about rest and relaxation. Rather than taking any time in Havana, Chevita took the resort shuttle directly from the airport to the Marbella Beach Resort. Chevita's plan consisted of lying on the beach reading the newest book in her favorite book series, having some cocktails, and meeting some interesting people. Chevita had a great first week at the resort. The weather was perfect, and the vacation was going exactly as she had planned. The one thing Chevita did not account for is how bad she was at relaxing; by Friday she was ready to explore the country. It was not in her personality to sit on the beach for two straight weeks, she needed to get out and do something. She did not know what was in the cards, but she knew she had to get out of the resort and see the real Cuba.

After four days of lying on the beach, Chevita rented a car from her resort on Friday and spent several hours driving all through Cuba. She was a little surprised at the amount of widespread poverty throughout the island. She knew that before the revolution that the average annual income of a family in Cuba was only $10,000, but she had hoped that for the five years since the revolution that life would have gotten better. She noticed some new businesses, but the majority of the people still lived in poverty. The juxtaposition of the dramatically elegant Marbella Beach Resort set among a country of such poverty was staggering. Chevita hoped things were different in Havana, so she planned to visit the capital on Saturday.

Havana had always been a charming city even before the revolution, so Chevita was excited to explore the city for the first time since the revolution. What she encountered was much of the same. She was shocked, how has it been over five years since the revolution, but there was very little change in the Cuban capital? She also was surprised by the large American soldier population in the capital. It did not feel as though the world was getting the whole story on Cuba, even on vacation Chevita had the hardest time turning off her work.

Chevita kept her room at the Marbella Beach Resort, but rather than traveling back she decided to live like a local; well at least a wealthy local, for that Saturday. She booked a room at the El Capitan in Havana for Saturday night. She decided she would go out for dinner and drinks, and see if she could meet any captivating people to get the true story of what life was like in Havana since the revolution. She would not treat the night as if she were covering a news story, but based on what she had seen for the past two days Chevita believed that at some point Cuba would once again become a hot news topic. Her night on the town might just lead her to a good story when she starts her new job at NNC.

All of Chevita's clothes were back at the Marbella Beach Resort, so rather than waste time by trekking all the way back, she decided to take the afternoon to go shopping in one of the only upscale areas of Havana, Las Olas. Chevita's Cuban blood and fluency in Spanish allowed her to fit in as a local anywhere she went in Havana, and with her outgoing personally she quickly met friends. While shopping in one of the boutiques, a saleswoman in her mid-twenties named Isabella invited Chevita to join her and a group of her girlfriends for a night out at the city's hottest salsa club, Café Cintron. Isabella laid out the perfect dress and shoes for her, and after trying them on Chevita was thrilled for her night out with new friends. Chevita had been so focused on work since graduating college that she did not have many nights out with friends back in Miami, she did not have a boyfriend, and until now she did not realize how lonely her life really was. She had multiple acquaintances in Miami, was well loved and respected, but she had sacrificed so much for her career. Chevita vowed to herself that she would keep in mind that there is more to life than work when she started her new job in Washington DC.

Although everyone thought Chevita was gorgeous, she typically held a very humble opinion of her looks. She did not understand why she was considered to be pretty, beautiful, hot, sexy, whatever she was called, but tonight was different. When Chevita slid into her tight yet flowing new coral dress and looked into the mirror, she finally saw what others had been saying about her for years. Her confidence going to meet her new friends at Café Cintron was at an all-time high. She danced with the girls to a few songs, and although she and Isabella hit it off immediately some of her friends were not quite as fond of the attention that Chevita was receiving. After a couple of songs Chevita retreated to the bar while having a mojito alone, Isabella came over to check on Chevita.

"How is everything going over here? Are you having fun?"

"I'm having a great time, thank you so much for inviting me out. I'm not sure if you friends like me though?"

"Don't worry about them, they are just jealous, look at you, you're beautiful."

"Thanks, you're making me blush."

"Come on you must get that all the time, so what's your story, what brought you to Havana?"

"I'm in between jobs back in the states, and I thought I would go on a vacation"

"Nice, where are you staying?"

"The Marbella Beach Resort."

"Wow, beautiful with money, so where's your husband?"

"Haha, I don't have a husband."

"You will make some man very happy one day."

"Really? Aww you're so sweet. You are pretty awesome yourself. All the guys in Cuba must be all over you."

About this time the man sitting to their left looks over curious about where this conversation is heading. He shakes his head and orders a Havana Club and Ginger from the bartender. Isabella notices it is her cousin, and takes the opportunity to change the subject that is quickly becoming a little awkward.

"Heyyyy, Javy, this is my new friend Chevita," Isabella says with a wink.

"Hello Chevita, nice to meet you," he says trying to be cool, but incredibly nervous.

"Very nice to meet you as well Javy."

"Can I buy you a drink?"

"Sure, I am just having a mojito."

"Typical, I'll get you a mojito."

"Typical, what does that mean, is that supposed to be sexist?"

"No, I just mean that every American that comes to Havana wants to try a real mojito and smoke a Cuban cigar."

Chevita thought back to the conversation she had with her father about Americans having a new place to vacation and better cigars to smoke. She was intrigued by Javy's honesty, and found herself biting her lip between questions.

"How did you even know I was American, am I that obvious?"

"Yes, but I forgive you," Javier said with a chuckle.

"You're much more cute when you keep your mouth shut, why don't you ask me to dance."

"Nope, I don't dance."

"What kind of Cuban doesn't salsa dance?"

Chevita proceeds to drag Javy onto the dance floor. He is actually a phenomenal dancer. Chevita had not had this much fun in a long time.

"Wow you really can dance, why would you lie about that."

"Maybe I didn't want you to want me anymore than you obviously already do."

"Pshhh, you wish that were the case, maybe I just wanted someone to dance with."

The friendly banter is turning into heavier and heavier flirting, the sexual tension quickly boils over, and this time Javy makes the first move, kissing Chevita. Isabella looks over, giving her cousin a smile; it's nice to see him break out of his shell. Chevita is smitten, before she knows it she is leaving with Javy.

When the morning light began to peak through the curtains of Chevita's hotel room she looks to her left she sees a man she realizes she does not even know. She immediately smacks her forehead, embarrassed by her behavior, and the realization that this trip was more like her Cancun Spring Break than she thought it would be. She did not even know this man's last name, and now he was lying in bed next to her. Even though she was embarrassed by her behavior, she was intrigued with the evident chemistry between her and Javy, and rather than make a bad situation worse, she decided to get to know him. When Javy woke up much to his disappointment Chevita was already dressed. Javy was thinking, "wow, how did I manage to win over this beautiful woman, what do I do now?" Rather than over thinking the situation, Javy decided to lighten the mood by offering to take Chevita to brunch. Chevita accepted but only under the condition that she would do the driving and pick the place.

"This is where I'm really staying for my two weeks in Cuba. It's all inclusive, so brunch is on me."

"Wow, this is how the other half lives. I've never seen anything like this."

"It's really no big deal. I hope you are ok with joining me for the day?"

"Absolutely I couldn't think of a better way to spend the day."

Chevita and Javy enjoy brunch, followed by a day on the beach. While lying on the beach they really start to get to know each other.

"So what is your full name?"

"Javier Hernandez." Javier does not think that Chevita will have any idea of his background.

"Really, come on, you are still going to give me a fake name after last night and today?"

"That's really my name," Javier could tell that Chevita knew his story. "I was hoping being American that you would not know who I was."

"I knew I recognized you, I just did not know how. I'm actually a news reporter, and I covered many of the stories behind the Cuban Revolution."

"Where do you work?"

"Well, I did work for News Channel 13 in Miami, but I just took a new position at NNC out of Washington DC."

In some ways Javier likes Chevita even more based on their conversation, but he also knows this likely means what they will never be more than a vacation fling. Chevita realizes just how much her life is going to change, but decides to not stress the future and to enjoy her time with Javier.

"You know I always wanted to meet you, I can't believe here you are lying on a beach beside me."

"Haha, thanks, hope I was not too much of a letdown."

"Are you kidding me? Not at all."

Now it appears that their fling is turning into a little more than a one night ordeal. They are both starting to have feelings for each other, which seems out of character and absolutely ridiculous to both of them. The two of them spend the entire week together, while Javier's parents watch Orlando. Javier and Chevita have an amazing week together; it is a shocking surprise considering where they are both at in life, but worth every minute.

The two week vacation went so much differently than Chevita ever thought it would, but it was exactly what she needed. Chevita was able to relax and rejuvenate her soul before starting her challenging new job in Washington DC. She was also able to experience life in Cuba and make what could be some very valuable contacts in Havana between Isabella and Javier. Most importantly Chevita was able to reevaluate her life priorities, and realize that there is more to life than working all the time. By the end her stay, Chevita and Javier were able to realize that it is going to be very difficult to maintain any type of long distance relationship between Washington DC and Cuba, but they vow to keep in touch.

Chapter 11

Baseball has long been the national sport of Cuba and even more than that it is has been an escape for the people throughout years of hardship. The Havana Knights have sold out their 30,000 seat stadium for every game for over thirty years. After the embargo and travel restrictions were lifted to Cuba in 2020, a group of investors led by former major league players and major league owners decided to cash in on the popularity of baseball in Cuba. This group of investors decided to resurrect the Baseball World Cup, and to hold the first Baseball World Cup in Havana in November of 2025. The Baseball World Cup was originally held from 1938-2011, with Cuba winning the most gold medals of any nation at 25. Cubans have always been proud of their baseball accomplishments, so Havana was the perfect place to hold the first Baseball World Cup in fourteen years. The only differences would be that this year each nation would send their best players, professional or amateur, to play for their respective countries with the reward being national pride, and a two million dollar per player purse to the champion of the two week long tournament. The two million dollar per player purse was enough to attract the best players in the world to play in the two week tournament. The combination of such high levels of talent and the ratings often associated with international events such as the Olympics, World Cup, and the Champions

League, helped the investors secure a ten-year, multi-billion dollar deal with a major television network to broadcast the Baseball World Cup around the world.

Javier's career for the past five years has been as the public address announcer for all of the Havana Knights baseball games. When it was announced that Havana would host the 2025 Baseball World Cup in the Havana Knights' stadium Javier was naturally selected to also be the public address announcer for the tournament. Javier had developed friendships with many of the Cuban players from his time as the Havana Knight's announcer, and he was excited to be able to see them play against the best players in the world.

After the June 28th meeting, the "Javier Twelve" led non-violent protests throughout all of the squares in Havana. Their efforts caught on rapidly, and what started as protests of twenty grew to protests of 200, then to protests of 2000. The local news began to cover the protests, but the story had yet to gain traction internationally. Javier's plan was coming together, and thanks to the original "Javier Twelve" he knew he had the support of Cuba to make a change.

Roughly half of the players on the Cuban National Team for the 2025 Baseball World Cup played in the Cuban Professional League, with the other half playing in the Major Leagues. Even the players in the Major Leagues started off in the Cuban Professional League, so Javier knew everyone on the team, and everyone on the team had a tremendous amount of respect for Javier for what he had done for Cuba. The players on the Cuban National Team were extremely proud to represent Cuba for the first time since the fall of the oppressive regime.

Going into the tournament the United States team was the favorite, with the Cuban team holding the number two seed. Throughout the early rounds both teams lived up to the hype, and on November 15, 2025 the two met in the finals set in the Havana Knights stadium. The Cuban National Team was actually the favorite in the final because of the home town backing. The morning before game one of the best of three series, Javier approached the team in the locker room before batting practice. The team held such respect for Javier that when he walked into the locker room, there was immediate silence in anticipation for what he was about to say.

"I want each of you to know that the people of Cuba are extremely proud of you, and I am one of your biggest fans. I consider myself lucky to know what great people each of you are off the field. You are all amazing players, and I am sure you can defeat any opponent that stands in your way. I am coming to you today for a cause bigger than baseball. You have the opportunity to make a statement to the world today. Each of you are competitors, you would not be here if you were not, so I know what I am going to ask of you will not be easy. As many of you know there have been protests on every square throughout Cuba for the last few months. I trust each of you enough to let you know that I am behind each of those protests. These protests are making it on the local news, but they have yet to make it to the international news. It is time for Cuba to be truly free, and I need your help to bring attention to the cause. Today's game will be broadcast around the world. It is estimated that roughly 200 million viewers will tune in for your match up against the United States. This is the perfect stage to make a statement. The decision is yours. Your statement can be, 'we are the best baseball team in the world,' or your statement can be, 'Cuba needs your help, we deserve our independence.' If you decide that you would rather use this stage to make a statement for Cuba, this is my plan, and I hope you are on board. It has been over six years since, Dia de La Revolucion Finale on June 26, 2019, and every day we celebrate that day just outside of this stadium in Plaza Vieja. What are we truly celebrating? We are not really free, sure we have more freedom than we did before the revolution, but we still have thousands of American troops policing us, and infringing on our freedoms every day. Typically the 27th or last out of the game is the most important, but today the 26th out is going to be the most important out. I need each of you to make a statement in honor of Dia de La Revolucion Finale, and to show the world the truth about Cuba. After the 26th out, or the second out in the bottom of the ninth inning, I want each of you to walk off the field. This move will create sheer confusion in the stadium, and the television announcers will have no option, but to broadcast the events taking place. At this point I will come in over the PA and explain to the world the situation in Cuba that has been neglected for too long."

The room fell silent for ten seconds, but in that intense moment it felt more like ten minutes. Each of the players were thinking about this moment and what it would mean both to them personally, to Cuba, and to the world. After ten seconds, Livian Roca, the captain and starting pitcher, of game one spoke up.

"Javier, I am with you, if I am blessed enough to pitch 8-2/3 innings tonight, I will walk off the field after we record the 26th out."

About this time there was some resistance from some of the younger, lesser paid, players.

"Do you realize what you are asking of us? If we win this series we will be paid two million dollars, but if we lose we get nothing! That amount of money can be life changing, we have not made it to the Major Leagues, and there is no guarantee that we will," three rookies exclaimed.

"I do realize that, but no amount of money can change the world or buy happiness," Javier responded.

About this time the remaining 21 players on the team stood up with Livian Roca, and agreed that they would execute Javier's plan. Reluctantly the three rookies joined. The support of the Cuban National Team left Javier in tears.

"You do not know what this means to me, and to the people of Cuba. I'm sure at some point each of you have been called a hero, well your actions tonight will be truly heroic. Thank you."

The energy felt in Havana due to the anticipation of the showdown between Cuba and the United States in the 2025 Baseball World Cup was staggering. There was a sold out stadium of 30,000 fans with 100,000 or more people outside the stadium just wanting to be as close to the action as possible. There were another 200 million people tuned in around the world, many of which were not even baseball fans, but rather just intrigued with the story of Cuba against the United States.

The game itself was as exciting as expected. Cuba went up to an early 2-0 lead, with a home run by Raul

Esteban in the top of the first inning. Livian Roca pitched flawlessly over the first six innings, scattering four hits without allowing a run. Cuba was in trouble in the bottom of the seventh when Derrick Smith cleared the bases for a three-run home run to give the United States the lead. During a visit to the mound Livian was able to convince his coach that he was fine and that he wanted to pitch the complete game. Cuba fought back in the top of the ninth when, Alex Cora singled in two runs to set up the bottom of the ninth. The lead-off man for the United States singled, and then stole second, setting up a man in scoring position without anyone out. Now the trouble with Javier's plan was the United States' best hitters were due up, with the winning run at the plate. A home run would end the game before Livian could even get to the 26th out. Livian stared in at the catcher, when the nervousness got to him. He stepped off the mound and immediately threw up in the infield. Livian had pitched in countless high pressure games, but he never had the opportunity to make a difference the way he did tonight. He knew he had to buckle down. With adrenaline running through his veins, Livian was able to reach back and give everything he had for the next 8 pitches, hitting a high of 98 on the radar gun. That type of power is unheard of in the ninth inning for a starting pitcher. Livian struck out the next two batters, threw his fist in the air and walked off the field. The rest of the team followed him, one out from winning game one of the Baseball World Cup. The Cuban National Team had achieved the goal they set out to accomplish. Livian pointed up to Javier in the press box, and shouted; "Now it's on you."

"I would like to speak to the people here in Cuba, and more importantly to the viewing audience around the world. You are probably wondering why the Cuban National Team would walk off the field when they were only one out away from winning game one of the Baseball World Cup, and half way to a two million dollar per player prize. Cuban's are prideful and determined; we are willing to make a stand for what we believe in no matter the circumstance. Dia de La Revolucion Finale took place on June 26, 2019, now six years later we are still not truly free. There are thousands of American soldiers throughout Cuba. Why are they still here? I fought for our freedom in the Cuban Revolution, my wife died for our freedom, and now I am raising our child in a Cuba that is being ruled by the United States military. We were promised an independent nation with the plan being for temporary assistance from the United States to establish a true democracy, but that is not what we have received. We do not want to start a war, we do not want to see any bloodshed, we just want our freedom. The power lies with you the viewer, we need you to be the change, we need you take a stand up for us and for human rights in Cuba. Contact your representatives in Congress, stay up on current events, and go out and vote. We cannot do it alone, we need your help. Thank you, and good night."

The crowd was in shock.   After the initial silence the crowd erupted, with the chants of "Free Cuba!" and "Javier for President!" The point was made, and now all they could do was hurry up and wait. Javier had not broken any laws created in the Diplomatic Agreement of 2019 between the United States and Cuba, so he did not feel as if he was in any jeopardy of being jailed. He walked home, and prayed for change.

Chapter 12

After returning from Cuba, Chevita felt reenergized and ready to start her new career with NNC in Washington DC. She arrived in Washington DC on October 20th, so she would have nearly two weeks to get ready for her new position and adjust to a new city. Washington DC was so much different than Miami, and Chevita could tell within the first week that she was going to have an adjustment period. The weather was much colder, national politics was always a hot topic, and the people were much more cutthroat and willing to do whatever it took to move up the corporate ladder. It was not at all the environment she was accustomed to, and while she knew that when she accepted the position with NNC, Chevita was in culture shock her first month in DC.

On her first day at NNC Chevita met her team. It was the first time in her life she felt like "a nobody." In Miami she was a local celebrity with her image plastered on billboards, and even when she was a child her well established parents always included her in all of Miami's top social events. In Washington DC, no one knew her name or her past accomplishments nor did they care. She realized very quickly she was going to have to work hard and grind her way through the corporate scene to make an impact. Her first story was on the Vice President, James Gamble's, daughter's Sweet 16 birthday party. Chevita was embarrassed, and she felt like a laughing stock. It was within the first week that Chevita had her first altercation with her executive producer, Nick Jameson.

"I thought my position was going to be as the lead field reporter for the upcoming Presidental election," a frustrated Chevita complained to her executive producer.

"It is, Vice President Gamble is running for President, it is important for the public to know what type of man they may or may not be voting for. Besides it makes for good ratings." Nick Jameson responded

"I do not understand how his daughter's birthday party hosted by 'some rap star' has anything to do with the upcoming election, shouldn't we be more concerned with informing the public of his political views. Besides I have veto power over which stories I will cover."

"I'm not sure who gave you veto power, but he is not in charge here, I am. If you want to do a story on the Mr. Gamble's political views, then you need to do the leg work and make it happen. I don't know how your job worked where you came from, but at NNC we are not going to just hand you a story on a silver platter. This is Washington DC, and you are supposed to be our lead field reporter, start acting like it."

Chevita left the conversation with her executive producer angry and frustrated, not just at Nick Jameson, but at herself. She felt like she was already making a bad name for herself, and she had not even been with NNC for a week. She wanted to call her parents, but she did not want them to worry about her. She wanted to call Javier, but she did not want to come off as weak to such a strong man. She knew what she had to do. She had to step up and land a big story on the Presidential candidates for the 2026 Election. That was going to be the only way to gain respect in such a cutthroat town.

Chevita started talking to all the right people, and really getting an in with the two leading Presidential candidates, Current Vice President James Gamble, and current Senator Jordan Franklin. James Gamble rode into Washington on the coat tails of President Morgan, it was known that he swayed more liberal in his political views, but not much was really known about how he thought the country should be ran. Conversations with Vice President Gamble were typically very light in nature. He shied away from controversial political issues, and tended to divert the focus onto light hearted social issues such as family life, politically incorrect sports team names, legalizing or decriminalizing recreational marijuana. Senator Franklin was just the opposite, he was outspoken as an ultra-conservative voice in the Senate. Everyone knew where Jordan Franklin stood on all the pressing issues in 2026, and around a third of people in the country loved him, a third hated him, and a third did not care enough about politics to know the difference. Senator Franklin did not possess the charm or public speaking skills of Vice President Gamble, so naturally Vice President Gamble was more popular with the average American in late 2025. Chevita admired the Vice President as a man, but she wanted to know more about his policies and his vision for the future of the United States. She found it as her duty as a news reporter to inform the American public of the truth so that they could make an educated decision on the future of the United States.

On November 15, 2025 after her second week at NNC, Chevita was sitting alone in her apartment flipping through the channels on Saturday night when she stumbled across the Cuba vs United States Baseball World Cup game. She was intrigued with the game because of her time in Cuba just last month. Baseball was not all that interesting to her, so naturally her thoughts wandered to Javier, and their steamy Havana nights. Chevita caught herself biting her lip, and daydreaming about Javier when the game took a sudden turn. She watched as Livian Roca struck out the clean-up hitter for the United States for the second out in the bottom of the ninth inning and walked off the field with his fist held high. The rest of the team followed him off the field much to the bewilderment of the crowd and the commentators. Suddenly Chevita felt butterflies in her stomach as the man she had just been daydreaming about appeared on her screen. Javier explained to the world how Cuba needed their help to become an independent nation, and how the United States military occupation had gone on for too long. Chevita was so proud of Javier, but she was also concerned. Would he be arrested or killed for his rebellious move, or would the people of Cuba protect him?

Suddenly Chevita had an epiphany. That was her story; she needed to find out more about what was going on in Cuba, and how that affected the United States. Now that Javier made his stand, and refocused the world's attention on Cuba this would surely be a topic for the upcoming Presidential election. Maybe she could even use Javier in a story. Chevita, stopped and thought about it for a minute, was this a good story, or was she looking for an excuse to see Javier? It could be both, right? Chevita decided to proceed with the story on Cuba, hoping this would be her big break at NNC.

Chapter 13

The next Monday Chevita presented the idea of further examining the situation in Cuba to her executive producer. Initially Nick was not impressed, but Chevita was able to make her case.

"I guess I do not really understand what Cuba has to do with the United States, and especially the upcoming Presidential election. There are so many more important stories than Cuba going into this election. Maybe in Miami people care about what is going on in Cuba, but we do the national news, and I do not see how this story appeals to a national audience. This is really the first story you want to pitch to me?"

Chevita ignored his seemingly rhetorical question, "We have had thousands of troops in Cuba for over six years, do you not find that odd? Think about the tax money alone that we are spending to maintain a presence in Cuba. I do not know if you watched the Baseball World Cup on Saturday night or not, but the entire Cuban National Team walked off the field in a protest, and the announcer, Javier Hernandez, former leader of the revolution, made an announcement to the international viewing audience pleading for help to remove the United States military. The people of Cuba do not even want the American military there. Cuba should have been an independent country years ago, but somehow a semi-militaristic state has been created, that we the American tax payers are bankrolling. There are so many questions that need to be answered. Why is the US military still in Cuba? What are we hoping to accomplish there? How much longer will we maintain a presence? Who is maintaining this presence? I want to provide our viewers with these answers, so they can make informed voting decisions going into next year's election."

"I don't love the idea, but you have made valid points. I will allow it, but don't let me down."

That afternoon Chevita made a call to her strongest contact for the story, Javier. Chevita was nervous making the call, but she thought the call should not come as a surprise as she had left Cuba nearly a month prior vowing to keep in touch.

"Hi, this is Chevita, sorry to call you out of the blue."

"No need to apologize, it is so good to hear from you, how are you?"

"I'm doing well, just making the transition to life in Washington DC. I saw you during the game on Saturday, how is everything going there?"

"Oh you saw that, I guess that is good that the message go out to the world. Things are hectic here, everything is a little crazy. I have stayed in the house, I know I did not break any laws, but I am still nervous to get thrown in prison."

"I was hoping I could help you and Cuba. I plan on trying to get some more answers from the politicians here in Washington, and from the military leadership in Cuba. I want to present the story to the entire nation later this week."

"Oh, that's why you were calling. That sounds great, let me know what I can do to help."
"What do you mean? That's why I was calling."

"I just hoped that you were calling to catch up, or make plans to come see me."

"Ok.....I'm just really trying to make a name for myself at NNC, I would love to see you again, but I have not thought that far ahead. I thought you would just be happy to hear from me, and that we could have a mutually beneficial agreement for this story."

"I'm sorry, you are right, I felt like I made it awkward now. Can we just focus on the story?"

"I like that plan, besides, maybe I will get a business trip to Cuba out of this story, and you know what that means."

"That would be perfect, if only we could be so lucky. Anyway for now we should focus on the story. As far as Cuba goes, General Wallace is in charge here, but he is a bit of a recluse. He has not actually been seen in Havana for years. The visible leader and General Wallace's second in charge is Bo Vance. He is very involved on the ground level for such a high ranking military officer, and as much as I hate him, I think he is your best contact to find out what is really going on."

"Why do you hate him?"

"He has made a point to show his power. He even tried to make an example of me by arresting me in front of my son. That led to a public uprising during the Dia de la Revolucion Finale celebration this past summer. Bo Vance ended up in the hospital after being knocked unconscious from a flying stone, and I ran home with Orlando. After that day it was clear that change was needed in Cuba, and that the United States military welcome was wearing thin. After that I assembled a group of twelve brave men to lead non-violent protests in every square in Havana for the next few months. That led to Saturday night's events during the Baseball World Cup. After I knew the people of Cuba truly wanted an independent government I felt comfortable to lead the protest at the game. "

"I never heard that story, why did you not tell me about that when I was in Cuba with you?"

"Because I was just trying to get to know you, and I did not want work to get in the way of your vacation. I think we had a great time because of it."

"I guess you are right, so how do you suggest I get ahold of Bo Vance?"

"Call the JCOMMCARIBCOMMAND headquarters in Havana, and they will get you in touch with Bo. Do not let them know I was your contact to talk with him, or you will not get anywhere."

"Thanks Javier, I appreciate the information." Chevita really wanted to say I miss you, but she refrained.

"You're welcome, maybe I will get to see you soon."

"I hope so, stay safe down there."

The next day Chevita called JCOMMCARIBCOMMAND, and surprisingly Bo Vance answered the phone. It turned out his punishment from General Wallace for his stunt with Javier was to have office duty once a week for the rest of the year.

"JCOMMCARIBCOMMAND, Bo Vance speaking, how may I help you sir or mam?"

"Hello my name is Chevita Diaz, and I am calling on behalf of the National News Corporation. I am a field reporter for the nightly news, and you are just the man I was hoping to talk to. Would you be willing to answer some questions on the United States military's involvement in Cuba?"

Bo Vance cautiously looked around the room, as he has wanted to talk with a reporter on what was going in Cuba, but was afraid of the repercussions. "I am willing to hear what you have to say, but I cannot confirm or deny any plans of the United States military."

"How many troops are currently occupying Cuba?"

"7500"

"That is a 50% increase from what was agreed upon in 2019, why has there been an increase?"

"I cannot answer that question."

"Very well, what is the plan moving forward in Cuba?"

"As I said I cannot confirm or deny any plans of the American military."

"Very well, can I ask your opinion on the United States involvement in Cuba."

"I am not allowed to express my opinion on any matters on our involvement in Cuba."

"Well it sounds as though this interview is not going anywhere, thank you for your time, I will let you go. Be safe down there."

"Thank you, have a good day mam, and good luck with your story."

Chevita was frustrated, how was she supposed to get anywhere with the information she collected. She knew that her executive producer would likely be asking about her story within the next day, and currently she had nothing to present to him. She feared the story may be cut. She decided to move on to calling the political offices of both of the Presidential candidates. She started with Senator Jordan Franklin's office.

"Senator Franklin's office, how may I help you," answered his assistant.

"Hello my name is Chevita Diaz, and I am calling on behalf of the National News Corporation. I have been assigned to cover the upcoming 2026 Presidential election. Would you be willing to answer some questions on the United States military's involvement in Cuba?"

"I can tell you that Senator Franklin does not support any of the foreign policies of the current administration or of his opponent in the upcoming Presidential race."

"Thank you for that information, but I was hoping for answers to more specific questions."

"I am not in a position to answer any specific questions in regard to Senator Franklin's views on Cuba."

"Could I schedule an interview with Senator Franklin?"

"Senator Franklin is a very busy man, as he is on the campaign trail, and with the holidays approaching his earliest availability is not until into the New Year."

Chevita knew that was not going to be acceptable for her story that was supposed to air in three days, but she also knew how difficult it was to gain an interview with a Presidential candidate. Chevita planned an interview with Senator Franklin for January 11, 2026. Even though she would not be able to use the interview for her story on Cuba, Chevita considered landing the interview a victory for her new career.

After talking with Senator Franklin's office, Chevita contacted Vice President James Gamble's office.

"Vice President Gamble's office, how may I help you," answered his assistant.

"Hello my name is Chevita Diaz, and I am calling on behalf of the National News Corporation. I have been assigned to cover the 2026 Presidential election. Would you be willing to answer some questions on the American military's involvement in Cuba?"

"I can tell you that Vice President Gamble fully supports the foreign policies of the current administration."

"Thank you for that information, but I was hoping for answers to more specific questions."

"I am not in a position to answer any specific questions in regard to Vice President Gamble's views on Cuba."

"Could I schedule an interview with the Vice President?"

"Vice President Gamble is a very busy man, as he is on the campaign trail, and with the holidays approaching his earliest availability is not until into the New Year."

Chevita was surprised at how mirrored the conversations were with Senator Franklin office and Vice President Gamble's office. She grew even more suspicious, why was it so difficult to get an answer to her most basic questions. Once again she knew that waiting until the New Year to speak with the Vice President was not going to be acceptable for her story that was supposed to air in three days, but she also knew how difficult it was to gain an interview with a Presidential candidate. Chevita planned an interview with Vice President Gamble for January 9, 2026. Chevita had not gotten anywhere with Bo Vance, but she had landed interviews with both major Presidential candidates.

The next morning before Chevita could even shut the door to her office, Nick Jameson confronted her on the status of her story in Cuba. It was already Wednesday, and the story was supposed to be ready for the Friday evening newscast. Seeing her executive producer first thing in the morning when she was behind on a story was not the way Chevita wanted to start her day.

"So how is the story on Cuba coming?"

"Good, I have interviews lined up with Vice President Gamble, and Senator Franklin. Also, I spoke with one of the head military officers in Cuba."

"Wow, I'm impressed, so when are your interviews with Vice President Gamble and Senator Franklin?"

"They are in January. That was the earliest I could schedule the interviews."

"How are you going to do a story without those interviews? What about the conversation with the military officer in Cuba, did you get any information out of that?"

"I found out the number of troops in Cuba has increased by 50% to 7500 from the 5000 that was agreed upon in 2019."

"Anything else?"

"I'm still working on it."

"You have nothing, I'm happy to hear you have interviews with the Presidential candidates, but it is now Wednesday and we have a segment to run on Friday. I think it is best for us to cancel this segment until January. Your segment will now be on the litter of labradoodle puppies had by President Morgan's dog in the Whitehouse last week."

Chevita felt defeated, what was it going to take to gain the level of respect she had in Miami at her new position in Washington DC? She set up interviews with Presidential candidates, did her homework on the situation in Cuba, and contacted all the right people. Sure the story was not working out as quickly as expected, but it was turning into a better story by the day. That night Chevita received the phone call that would change her life.

"Hello, could I speak to Chevita?"

"This is she, who is this?"

"Bo Vance, we spoke briefly yesterday about the US military presence in Cuba."

"Yes, thank you for calling me back. Would you like to change you position?"

"I need to speak to you in anonymity, as the repercussions of what I plan to tell you could be very serious."

"Anything you want to say is in total confidence, unless you decide otherwise."

"I mean it. I could be dishonorably discharged and thrown in prison if the wrong people find out. Even with the threat of jail time I feel it is my patriotic duty to tell you what is really going on in Cuba."

"You have my word, what would you like to tell me? I will not use your name unless you decide you are comfortable with coming forward."

"The situation in Cuba is much more serious than anyone realizes. I have been in Cuba for the last three years, and I have seen the military presence continue to grow. For the longest time I did not see any issue with our presence in Cuba, and I never questioned what we were doing there. I just followed orders, and did what I could to maintain order in Havana. I was promoted all the way to the number two ranking officer behind General Wallace in

Cuba. It was in June during the Dia de La Revolucion Finale celebration that everything changed. I let hubris get in the way of judgment. I made a big mistake that I believe may spark a secondary revolution. I attempted to arrest Javier Hernandez, the former leader of the revolution, on a rarely enforced law in an effort to make an example of him. In doing so, the crowd erupted, and to make a long story short I awoke the next day in the hospital while Javier was safe at home. Everything has changed for both me and for Cuba since that night. There have been numerous protests in Havana ever since, leading up to the Baseball World Cup walk out, and Javier's big announcement on international television. Tensions are very high here in Cuba, and rightfully so. After waking up in the hospital General Wallace came to see me, not to see if I was ok, but to make me aware of what a mistake I had made attempting to arrest Javier and to let me know my punishment. The plan was that I would maintain my rank and position, but I would be on office duty once a week throughout the rest of the year. Honestly General Wallace does not do much on a daily basis, he is always in his office with the door closed. He does not even answer his phone, so whenever anyone calls I answer the phone. I started to notice that every Tuesday that I worked Vice President Gamble would call. At first I did not realize who it was, he would only ask to speak to General Wallace and to tell him that James was on the line. After the third week of calls, I began to get suspicious. I then realized there was an air duct that runs from the men's bathroom to General Wallace's office, so after I would transfer the call to General Wallace I would go to the bathroom, and lock the door. If I stood on top of the toilet, I could hear the conversation between General Wallace and Vice President Gamble. Based on what I heard if Vice President Gamble is elected there are no plans to make Cuba a free country, the militant rule will just increase, and soon General Wallace is to be the militant ruler of Cuba. That is scary enough, but more importantly, it sounds as though there may be plans to enact a similar policy in the United States if Vice President Gamble is elected."

"What! What do you mean by that?" Chevita was shocked as this was a huge development. The second ranking military officer in Cuba was telling her not only that Cuba was going to be under militant rule, but that the United States was going to be under militant rule as well.

"It is difficult to tell based on only hearing half of the conversation, but everything I heard indicated that the plan would be for a military style rule in the United States with Vice President Gamble becoming the dictatorial leader."

"That could never happen, what about our checks and balances? What about the American people, how would they allow that to happen?"

"I know, but that will not stop him from trying if elected. It is difficult to measure the power of the President; through executive orders presidents have been gaining more and more power for years. If elected President Gamble may be defeated, but the trauma that would occur to our nation to get him out of office could be devastating. Overthrowing a leader rarely happens without a great deal of bloodshed, and I do not want to see that on American soil."

"I completely agree with you, all of this is shocking. I need to take some time to process this information. I will be in touch with you, and I will give you my word that I will do everything I can to prevent this from happening. Thank you for your courage and for serving our country"

Chapter 14

It was another restless night for Chevita after her conversation with Bo Vance. If what Bo said was true, she could not fathom what the future would be like for both the United States and for Cuba should Vice President Gamble win the upcoming 2026 Presidential election. Chevita knew that she had to act quickly, but she did not know how to begin.

While restlessly lying in bed, Chevita thought back to her conversation over dinner with her father in little Havana nearly six years ago. Her father told her that she needed to be open to any opportunities where she could make a difference, and that advice is what landed her at NNC. Chevita had begun to doubt her decision to move to Washington DC until she received the life changing call from Bo Vance. Frankly compared to her life in Miami she hated the weather, she hated the city, she could not stand her executive producer, and she felt like an outcast at NNC. Now that her story on Cuba was developing, for the first time in her life Chevita felt that God had led her to this point, all of her frustrations were behind her, and it was time for her make a difference in the world.

Even with the lack of sleep Chevita quickly hopped out of bed with excitement to start her story on Cuba. She knew that she would have to make a case to Nick to travel to Cuba to meet with Bo Vance and Javier directly. Chevita was nervous to ask Nick if she could travel to Cuba to speak to a source. When she presented the idea to Nick it went just as she expected.

"I need to travel to Havana to talk with a very credible source about a story involving the upcoming election, will you approve my travel?"

"You want to do what!? Did I hear you say that you want to travel to Cuba for a story on the upcoming election? You mean the upcoming United States Presidential Election that you are supposed to be covering in OUR NATION'S CAPITAL? What does a trip to Cuba have to do with the Presidential election in the United States? You better have a really good reason to bring such a ridiculous request to me."

"I received a call from a high ranking American military officer in Cuba stating that there are no plans for the United States to remove their troops and allow Cuba to become a free nation, and even more serious than that if Vice President Gamble is elected he will attempt to enact the same style militant rule in the United States."

"Wow, that seems a little farfetched, I can see the Cuba thing but not militant rule in the United States. Who is your source?"

"It would be unethical to reveal my source as I gave him my word that he could speak in anonymously."

"I am your executive producer, and I need you to give me your source."

"I will not give you my source until I clear it with that person."

"Fine! It sounds like this could become a huge story, so I do not want to be the one to keep it from our viewers. You can go."

"Thank you so much, I really appreciate it, and I will not let you down."

"And Chevita,"

"Yes"

"If this story does not materialize, I suggest you begin looking for another job, maybe if you are lucky Miami News 13 will take you back."

Chevita was now in jeopardy of losing her job after only being there for a month. She had already put an exorbitant amount of pressure on herself, as she knew this was the story of her career, but now if for any reason the story fell apart it could be the last story of her career. Chevita knew she had to nail this story for her future, for the future of Cuba, and most importantly for the future of the United States.

Chapter 15

After talking with Nick, Chevita knew she had to travel to Cuba, but she did not have much of a plan besides that. Chevita could feel the weight of the world on her shoulders, but with all of that pressure she could barely think. She thought the best thing to do was to lean on her connections in Cuba. Although she knew that Bo and Javier were adversaries they were now Chevita's most important allies. She would need to get them in a room together, so the three of them could team up to properly expose Vice President Gamble and General Wallace.

Chevita knew she had to act quickly so she could have her story fully developed in time for her January 9th interview with Vice President Gamble. She decided with the approval of her executive producer she had free reign to do whatever she could to make this story happen. The next morning, Friday, November 21, 2025 Chevita traveled to Reagan International Airport to book a last minute ticket to Havana.

Everything happened so quickly from the time that Bo called her on Wednesday night, to the time she left for Cuba on Friday morning that Chevita did not even have a chance to tell Javier she was coming to Cuba. She was so excited to see Javier, but vowed not to let her feelings for him get in the way of the story. On the plane she thought about how she would make this story come together.

Chevita decided the best place for her to stay was the Marbella Beach Resort she stayed at during her last trip to Cuba. It was the perfect location for her trip. The resort was secluded enough that she could truly relax and gather her thoughts, but it was close enough to Havana that she could travel into the city to investigate her story.

When Chevita arrived in Cuba, she immediately wanted to see Javier, but she was able to come to her senses before calling him. If she called Javier immediately upon arriving in Cuba, she would get too distracted and the story would suffer. Not to mention she would come across as desperate, and she did not want him to think that he held all the cards in their "relationship." Instead Chevita decided to first call Bo Vance, and asked if he could meet her face to face. At first he was reluctant, because everyone knew who he was in Havana and how would it look for him to be seen with a news reporter?

"Bo, I took what you said to heart, and I decided in order to really get to the bottom of this story I needed to travel to Cuba, are you willing to meet me?"

"I'm not sure if that is a good idea, I'm well known throughout Havana, and I do not want anyone to know I am in talks with a news reporter."

"I understand that completely, which is why I booked a room at the Marbella, an all-inclusive resort only a forty-five minute drive from Havana. It is a very secure, and the only way through the gate is to have a room or be a guest of someone with a room. Also, this is an odd request, but wear swim trunks."

"That sounds like a good plan. Why swim trunks?"

"We want you to look like a typical American tourist. If you show up in Camo even people at the resort will think something is up. Besides I want you to feel relaxed when you talk with me, and what is more relaxing then laying on the beach with a cold drink in your hand. I already let the gate guard know you were coming. Let me know when you get here, I will be waiting down by the beach."

"Wow, I like the sounds of this interview. It is unlike anything I have done before."

"It's not an interview. We are just talking, and working on a plan. See you soon."

"See you soon."

Now that Chevita had the meeting with Bo lined up, she was ready to reach out to Jaiver. Even though she was there for business, she thought it would not hurt to flirt a little first, so she sent him a picture message of her tan legs on the beach with the crystal clear Caribbean Sea in the background. Within minutes she had a response.

"Is this picture from your time in Cuba in October, why do you have to tease me like that?"

"Guess where I am?"

"You're just messing with me. I know you are just missing the warm Cuban sunshine."

"I'm sitting in the warm Cuban sunshine, so the only thing I'm missing now is you."

Javier was confused, how had she traveled to Cuba without letting him know? How was he supposed to respond? They had such a great time together when she was in Cuba in October, but they had barely talked since she left, unless it was about a story. Now all of a sudden after barely talking for over a month, she is a forty-five minute drive away, sending pictures of her on the beach, and saying that she misses him. He knew he would never understand women, but she was far too great of a catch to stay mad at her for long.

"Really, so now you miss me? Is that an invitation?"

"Absolutely, I'm back at the Marbella Beach Resort, I already let the guard know you were coming. Come see me on the beach, thanks to my Cuban skin I'll be the only tan one in a white bathing suit. Everyone else staying at the resort is just a sunburnt American or European."

"How were you so sure that I would meet you?"

"I'm not even going to answer that question, see you in an hour, and I will have a Pina Colada waiting for you."

Javier decided to just go with it, and besides hanging out at an all-inclusive resort for the day sounded much better than sitting around the house waiting for Orlando to get home from school. Javier called Orlando's grandparents to pick him up from school, just in case he ended up staying later than he planned.

The main reason that Chevita traveled to Cuba was to have a meeting with Bo and Javier to discuss the plan moving forward. That meeting was now set up, but the only catch was that neither Bo nor Javier realized the other would be there. Chevita was nervous at how the meeting would go, but she knew teaming up with Javier and Bo was her best chance to do this right. Originally she planned to have Javier and Bo sit down in a room to discuss a plan moving forward, but she decided the beach sounded like a much better plan. The beach was secluded, safe, and everyone is relaxed when they are on the beach. That was particularly important considering the past history between Javier and Bo.

Bo arrived to the Marbella Beach Resort about an hour before Javier. When he walked to the beach where he said he would meet Chevita, he did not even think about how to distinguish her from the other guests at the resort. Luckily she had done her homework, and she spotted him right away. Even in swim trunks he had that military look. Chevita called him over, and everything went well. They mostly just made small talk to get to know each other a little better. Chevita knew it was a stressful situation for everyone involved, and she did not want to get into talking about a plan moving forward until Javier arrived.

When Javier arrived, things did not go as smoothly as Chevita had hoped. Emotions were riding high for Javier when he pulled up to the resort. He had not seen Chevita in over a month, but if he were being honest with himself he had missed her every day since. Javier began to walk down the beach looking for his sexy, tan, Cuban girl in the white bikini. His emotions quickly changed from excitement to confusion when he saw Chevita sitting on the beach beside a sun burnt American man with a shaved head and sunglasses.

"Chevita, so good to see you, what's going on here? Who's your friend?"

"Javier, it is great to see you too, it's not what it looks like. He is actually just here to help us. I'm working on a big story, and I think we should all team up."

Javier had never seen Bo in anything other than Army fatigues, so he did not immediately recognize him, but that did not last long. Once Javier realized that the man talking to Chevita was Bo Vance his emotions quickly changed from excitement to confusion to anger.

"What is this? You ask me to come meet you at a romantic resort, and your plan was only to have me meet him. I cannot stand this guy," Javier shouted while pointing vehemently at Bo.

"I don't care for you too much either buddy. Chevita, I thought you asked me to meet you here so we could come up with a plan. I trusted that this meeting was only between you and me. You choose to gain my trust by tricking me into a meeting with Javier Hernandez."

"I'm out of here, have a nice life," Javier shouted.

"Me too, I'll work with another reporter," says Bo.

"Wait, wait, this story is really important for the future of Cuba, and for the future of the United States. I did not know any other way to get the two of you together, but it is important for the three of us to work together as a team. You have to trust me."

At that point it did not matter what Chevita had to say, she could not do anything to keep Bo and Javier from leaving.

"Women, I'll never understand them, they all seem crazy" Bo said to Javier.

"I was just thinking the same thing,"

"I want to apologize. I'm sorry man, we started on the wrong foot, but I want you to know I realized how screwed up I was in the past. My views on you and all Cubans were completely off base."

"Apology accepted. We all do things we are not proud of. What is all of this about anyway? I feel like I was blinded by my anger back there. If there is one thing I do know it is that Chevita would not have set up a meeting between you and me unless it was for a really good reason."

"It is a long story, want to grab a beer and I'll tell you about it? I'll get the first round," Bo said to Javier.

"I think we both need a beer after that, besides we might as well take advantage of driving out to this all inclusive resort. Thanks for the beer, Chevita."

It may not have gone the way Chevita had envisioned, but Javier and Bo made peace with their past. They walked over to the resort bar where Bo told Javier everything. Javier was shocked, but in a selfish way he was relieved. He knew this had instantly become a much bigger story than he had ever imagined. This story would gain the attention needed to produce change.

While Javier and Bo stormed off, Chevita's eyes filled with tears. She had only been in Cuba for a few hours and already she had ruined everything. She had likely lost her story, lost her job, lost what could be the love of her life, and lost the chance to make a positive change in the world. She was ready to give up when she moped herself to the resort bar. Javier saw Chevita sitting at the bar in a reflection on the window around the corner from where she sat, and he asked the bartender to pour her a shot.

"From the gentleman around the corner, he and his friend are celebrating their new partnership over a shot of whiskey, and they would like for you to join them," said the bartender while he poured Chevita a shot.

"That's weird, who does that, just because I'm sitting at the bar by myself does not mean I want to take a shot with two random guys in a hotel bar."

"They seem like nice guys, you should at least peak around the corner to have a look."

Chevita was shocked when she saw Javier and Bo, not only having a drink together, but carrying on and having a good time. She walked over with a sly grin. "How is it that guys can do that, be ready to fight one minute, and then be drinking buddies the next?"

"It sounds like you are just as confused by men as we are about women, but how about we all put the past behind us and take a shot together."

"We need to come up with a plan, but let's do that in the morning, tonight is all about having a good time together." Chevita said to the new team.

"I like that plan, there are some gorgeous women at this resort that need to meet Bo Vance," Bo said while staring at a woman passing by.

"I agree all the women here are beautiful, but I got my eye on one in particular," Javier said while staring at Chevita.

Chevita gave him a smile, "I'm sorry about earlier, can we put that behind us?"

"I'm already over it. You know I cannot stay mad at you for long."

It had not gone at all the way Chevita planned it, but somehow her, Bo, and Javier were now a team. It was strange how they had developed a friendship that night, but it was one that they would hold on to for the rest of their lives.

Chapter 16

When the sun peaked through the window on Saturday morning Chevita once again found herself lying in bed next to Javier. It was just like her last trip to Cuba, except for this time it felt completely different. Even though she had not seen him in over a month Chevita felt completely comfortable with Javier. They had picked up right where they left off, and while people use that expression all of the time it is rare to actually have that feeling with someone that you had only spent one week of your life with. Chevita knew she had to set some ground rules for herself. She could not let her feelings for Javier in any way influence her plan moving forward with her story.

Now that Bo and Javier had developed a friendship and agreed to forgive Chevita for her lack of tactfulness in arranging their meeting, the three of them were ready to sit down to discuss the plan moving forward. Once Javier woke up, Chevita sent Bo a text to meet them for breakfast by the resort's pool.

"I'm glad we all had a chance to let loose last night and have a good time getting acquainted. Today is all about this story, and figuring out what is going on between our countries," Chevita started the conversation.

"Agreed, what would you like to discuss first?" Bo asked.

"Now that we know we are all on the same side, does everyone feel comfortable moving forward?"

"Yes," Javier and Bo both convincingly responded.

"I want the three of us to work as a team, as I think each of us plays an important part in developing this story."

"No offense, Chevita, but I do not really care about your story. I care about maintaining freedom in the United States." Bo cut her off before she could finish explaining.

"Sorry Bo, I did not phrase that correctly, but to me the story is the best way to approach this problem. Exposing the plot of Vice President Gamble and General Wallace is our best chance to maintain freedom in the United States."

"I can agree with that, but how do you propose we do that?" Bo questions Chevita.

"Hold on, I have not even heard a mention of Cuba in this discussion, what is the plan for Cuba?" Javier interjects.

"I understand your concern Javier, but it is one in the same. If we can expose this plot, it should also expose the situation in Cuba, which could lead to Cuba becoming a free nation."

"I'm hearing a lot of should's and could's, we have been dealing with the United States for long enough, and I do not want to deal in should's and could's any longer. We will have our freedom one way or another."

Bo quickly interjects, "What is that supposed to mean?"

Chevita could see this conversation was quickly going in the wrong direction, and she knew she had to get everyone back on the same page before the tension boiled over into a conflict.

"Take it easy, we all need to be on the same team if this is going to work. All three of us have slightly different but very closely related objectives. Bo wants to fulfill his patriotic duty to maintain freedom in the United States, Javier wants Cuba to gain independence, and I want to fulfill my journalistic duty to inform the American public so that they can make an educated decision for the upcoming election. I can promise you that a national news story to expose the plan of Vice President Gamble and General Wallace is going to be the best way for all three of us to accomplish our objectives."

"She is right, I apologize for losing focus," Javier agrees.

"Me too, so how do you propose we proceed?"

"I will conduct a series of stories, with associated interviews. The first interview will be with Javier. He will give his story from the revolution until today, and discuss what he sees as the future of Cuba if nothing changes. This will gain the sympathy of the American public. We will conduct this interview on Thanksgiving night after football, because typically after their Thanksgiving feast, Americans are most sympathetic to the less fortunate. Javier are you on board?"

"If you think this is the best way to proceed I trust you."

"Thanks Javier. That is exactly what I was hoping to hear." Chevita turns to Bo. "After the Javier interview airs I will set up a live interview with you and General Wallace to offer the United States military's side of the story in early January sometime before the interview with Vice President Gamble on January 9th. Considering his level of involvement General Wallace should want to defend the United States military's presence in Cuba. I will ask very difficult questions in an attempt to catch the General in a lie. I will simply need you tell the truth and nothing more. I currently have an interview scheduled with Vice

President Gamble on January 9th, the focus on that interview will be the plan for Cuba, and we will work to expose his plot for the United States in that interview."

"Your plan sounds risky, but honestly I do not have a better idea. Let's roll with it."

"We still need to iron out all the details, but I am glad we have a plan moving forward. The most important thing to remember is that we need to stick together as a team. I will not be able to do this without either of you."

Chapter 17

Chevita woke up on Sunday, November 23rd with a smile on her face. She had only been in Cuba for two days, and with the help of Bo and Javier she had a plan for her news story. The biggest challenge she had to overcome in the next few days was to get the approval of her executive producer to air the story on Javier just five days from now on Thanksgiving evening. Based on her limited experience in dealing with Nick, Chevita decided her best bet would be to propose each story to him individually, rather than to discuss her entire plan with him. She had faith that her plan would come together. First Chevita would gain America's sympathy for Cuba by interviewing Javier. Then she would establish distrust of the United States military presence in Cuba by interviewing General Wallace and Bo Vance, and finally she would expose the plot of Vice President Gamble during his interview on January 9, 2026. The good news was Chevita knew that individually each news segment held enough importance to be approved by Nick, but the bad news was with her job already in jeopardy she knew she had to successfully present each segment in order to even have a chance to fully execute her plan. Chevita's biggest fear was if for any reason she lost her job she would not be able to tie the stories together to paint the full picture for the American public.

In order to present the best story Chevita decided that the Javier interview should be conducted in Cuba. They would walk through the streets of Havana together while discussing his story. She wanted to be able to present the story in such a way that the American viewer could imagine themselves living in Javier's shoes. She needed to sell Nick on this idea, and get the network to send a camera crew to Havana. After having breakfast, Chevita walked down to the beach to call Nick.

"Hey Nick, it's Chevita,"

"How is your story coming?"

"It is going great, I have set up an interview with Javier Hernandez, the leader of the Cuban Revolution in 2018-2019, and currently one of the most influential Cubans. That is actually why I am calling you. I need you to send down a camera crew. I plan to interview him while walking down the street in one of the rougher neighborhoods of Havana. I think this interview will really hit home with the American public that does not really understand what it is like to live in Cuba. I was hoping the story could air on Thanksgiving evening after the football games."

"I like it. I will send a camera team down tomorrow. Be prepared to shoot on Tuesday, so we can edit and have it ready for Thursday. I will have the camera guys call you when you they get in town."

"Wow, Really?"

"Yes, good work. I'm not always a hard ass, only when my reporters are not living up to their potential."

"Thanks so much!"

Chevita was so excited to tell Javier. She went back to her room, where he was still sleeping, and woke him up.

"Javier, wake up, it is already 9 o'clock."

"Leave me alone, it is Sunday, Why do Americans always want to work so much and wake up so early?"

"Wake up, I have great news."

"I'm up, I'm up, what is it?"

"I just received the go ahead to proceed with our interview. My executive producer is sending in a camera crew tomorrow, and we are going to conduct the interview while walking through your old neighborhood in Havana on Tuesday. It is going to air this Thursday."

"That is news worth waking up for. I cannot wait to share our story."

Chevita and Javier spent the rest of the day going over the interview with their toes in the sand. There was not any reason they shouldn't take advantage of the beautiful Caribbean weather while preparing for the interview. Chevita explained to Javier that in order to get the sympathy of the viewers that Javier would have to discuss topics that may be uncomfortable for him. Javier would discuss his childhood in Cuba, followed by the changes he saw when the United States began to loosen their restrictions to Cuba, then he would go into the revolution, and the killing of his beautiful wife that left him as a widower and single father to a young son. They would then go into the time since the revolution and the expectations of the agreement with the United States in 2019 compared to the reality in 2025.

Javier went back home to be with Orlando that evening. Chevita and Javier both agreed that it would be best if he spent time with Orlando while she prepared for the interview. Neither of them wanted their chemistry for one another to come through on camera during the interview. Surprisingly, Javier was not at all stressed about the interview. He knew his story would tell itself, all he had to do was trust Chevita and tell the truth. Chevita on the other hand was very stressed. She finally seemed to have gotten in good graces with Nick, and she did not want to let him down. She stayed up until the early morning hours of Monday preparing for her interview of

Javier. She knew she would not be able to sleep until she was fully prepared for the interview. Being prepared was the only way that Chevita knew to reduce her stress, and by the time she woke up Monday morning her stress was gone. She spent Monday relaxing on the beach until she picked up the camera crew at the airport that afternoon.

After the camera crew arrived Chevita went back into business mode. She immediately drove the camera crew through some of the worst neighborhoods of Havana to show them where they would be shooting. She did not want any surprises or objections on Tuesday. The camera crew was shocked at the poverty, vandalism, and most of all the number of American soldiers policing the streets. They were not thrilled to be shooting in a bad neighborhood, but they knew it would make for an excellent news segment.

When Tuesday rolled around everyone was prepared for Javier's interview with Chevita. It was impressive for Chevita to coordinate such an effort in such a short amount of time. Chevita and the camera crew picked up Javier from his beautiful home to drive him to the crime riddled neighborhood he grew up in where they would conduct the interview. Javier lived in a well-to-do section of town, but the story would not have the same effect on the viewer if it were filmed in his elegant living room as it would if it were filmed in one of the rougher neighborhoods where Javier spent is formidable years. Javier had moved into the nice home given to him by Governor Puig five years ago, but he still remembered his roots.

The interview could not have gone better. Chevita, Javier, and the camera crew arrived just before sunset, and walked down Javier's old neighborhood streets. Javier was a legend in the neighborhood. There were even murals of him and Vanessa graffitied on concrete walls. Four times in the course of the twenty minute interview Chevita and Javier were interrupted by thankful residents to shake his hand and take a picture. Another key to the interview was seen in the background. Over the course of the interview at least a dozen soldiers could be seen in the background carrying M-16's. Once aired, the interview would paint a picture of Javier's tragic story, and the story of Cuba for the American viewer. Through Chevita's interview of Javier, Cuba was going to have a voice in the United States for the first time in years, and after hearing Javier's story the American public would sympathize with Cuba's desire for freedom. It looked as though step one to achieving the goal of Chevita, Javier, and Bo was complete.

Chapter 18

After the interview Chevita and Javier had to say their goodbyes. Chevita boarded the plane, and made her way back to Washington DC. The flight to Washington DC left Chevita with a couple of hours to think about what was going on between her and Javier. It was clear that they had chemistry, but how long would that chemistry last with them living hundreds of miles apart? Neither of them knew now what the future would hold, but under the circumstances now was clearly not the right time in either of their lives to begin a long distance relationship. They were both exactly where they needed to be to help Cuba gain independence, and to protect the freedom of the United States. The same personality traits of drive, focus, and vision that created such great chemistry between them were the same personality traits that were keeping them apart.

After taking the early non-stop flight home to DC, Chevita decided to head into the office Wednesday afternoon to make sure everything was set for Javier's interview to air after the Thanksgiving football games the next day. Chevita knew the camera crew had emailed Nick the video footage immediately following the interview, so she was nervous as she walked into Nick's office to discuss the interview. As she stepped into his office, Nick started clapping, "I'm impressed, you crushed it in Cuba."

"Thank you, I'm glad you liked it," Chevita wanted to jump up and down with excitement, but she held off for the sake of professionalism.

"I can't believe you were able to put together such an impactful story in such a short amount of time. Your interview of Javier is going to make for excellent TV. The only bad news for you is my expectations for you have gone through the roof, so keep up the good work. As a reward take the entire four-day Thanksgiving weekend off."

Chevita could not wait for the interview to air. She knew the anticipation was going to make for an extremely long day on Thanksgiving. Rather than just sitting around her apartment all day waiting for the interview to air, Chevita decided to surprise her parents by taking the 6:00 AM flight to Miami on Thanksgiving morning. When she arrived at her parent's house mid-morning, her father was in the front yard watering the lawn with a blank stare. When he saw Chevita pulling up to the house, he immediately dropped the water hose which landed right on the handle causing water to spray up in the air. As they shared their first hug in months neither of them cared about the water spraying behind them. Emmanuel Diaz thought to himself, at this point it does not matter how the turkey turns out or who wins the game today, my baby girl is home, and this is going to be a great Thanksgiving.

They went inside to greet Chevita's mother, and she shared the great news about her interview airing tonight with both of them. Chevita was excited to spend the holiday weekend at home with her parents, and to watch the biggest interview of her two biggest supporters that night.

Unfortunately the excitement came to an abrupt end during the 1:00 game between the Lions and the Dolphins in Detroit. During the halftime show an explosion erupted in the stands on the fifty yard line directly behind the stage. The scene quickly turned to panic. The terrorists behind the bombing were able to strike fear into millions of households across the country in an instant, and at that point nothing else mattered. Chevita was thankful to be home with her family, but within thirty minutes of the bombing she received a call from Nick. He asked her to get on the next flight to Detroit to cover the story. Chevita knew she did not have a choice, and she arrived in Detroit at seven that evening. She met her camera crew at the scene of the horrific act, and they immediately started a live news segment. Chevita thought her story would be broadcasted nationwide on Thanksgiving night, but she never thought it would be on a terrorist attack in Detroit. That night she received a phone call from Javier.

"Are you ok? I was able to watch your report from Detroit online."

"I'm a little shaken up. It was a horrific scene, even when I arrived five hours after the bombing, but I'll be ok. My thoughts and prayers are just with the victims and their families."

"I'm sorry you had to go through that, I feel awful for the families."

"It just feels like we are never safe, you know?"

"Yeah, it is a crazy world we live in….so, I hate to bring this up, but what does this mean for our interview?"

"How can you even ask me that right now? Do you realize what I've gone through today?"

"I know, I know, that story needs to be heard, nothing has changed here in Cuba."

"Well everything has changed here, and I can't believe you would ask me about that. You called acting like you cared about me, but all you really cared about was getting your story aired."

"You are right. I'm so sorry. I have just been so focused on that interview. I can't believe I was so selfish, I'm sorry." All Javier heard on the other end of the line was silence. The damage had been done, he had hurt someone he cared about and he did not know what else to say.

"I don't know what else to say, Chevita, I will let you go. Take care and be safe."

"Thank you, bye."

Chapter 19

Chevita spent the next week in Detroit covering the bombing. It was now December, and since being hired by NNC over a month ago as the lead field reporter in Washington DC to cover the upcoming Presidential election, Chevita had spent a week in Cuba and a week covering a terrorism story in Detroit. Chevita was fortunate to learn at an early age that life never goes as expected, but even she was shocked at how the past month had gone both professionally and personally.

The story on the bombing in Detroit remained the lead story for several weeks. It was a life changing event in the United States, and it was the talk of the nation. For the first time since September 11, 2001, the United States had been attacked on their home soil. All of the focus of the country and the upcoming election had shifted to how the United States was going to respond to this act of terror. Chevita was forced to shift gears from Cuba and cover the story that had the biggest immediate impact in the United States.

Meanwhile nothing had changed in Cuba, and Javier's interview had yet to air. Chevita knew that although it would not be popular to divert the attention from the bombing, Javier's interview still needed to be seen. The future of the United States and Cuba hinged on Chevita executing the plan she, Javier, and Bo had developed. She still had the interview scheduled with Vice President Gamble for January 9th. She would need to set the wheels in motion by Christmas for the story to fully come together to expose Vice President Gamble during his interview, but it would be extremely difficult to convince Nick to air Javier's interview considering the severity of the events in Detroit. On December 20, 2025, Chevita walked into Nick's office to ask for him to air Javier's interview.

"Nick, I need you air Javier's interview Christmas night."

"Are you crazy? We have too many problems in our own country to care about what is going on in Cuba right now."

"Do not forget how important this story is; remember it could have an impact on more than just Cuba. There is a chance that we could have an entirely different type of government if the wrong candidate is elected. Now with the fear instilled in the American public from the terrorist attack we are at an even greater risk of losing our freedom. We cannot let terrorism control every facet of our lives or the terrorists win, we need to proceed with informing the American public on all of the issues in the upcoming election, or voters will only vote based on how each candidate plans to handle the terrorist attack. That plan is very important, but there are also other extremely important policies of each candidate that need to be presented to the voter."

"It was a great interview, but I just do not know how the public will react. Ok, it will air, but not on Christmas night. We will air it on Monday, December 29th."

"Thank you Nick, you will not regret this decision."

Chevita called Javier to let him know his interview was finally going to air. They had not spoken since Thanksgiving night, and although she was nervous to call him she knew it was the right thing to do.

"Hello"

"Chevita, it is so good to hear from you. How are you?"

"I was just calling to let you know that your interview is going to air on December 29th at 6:30 PM."

"Wow, that is great news, thank you so much for letting me know. Are you doing well?"

"I'm fine, like I said I just wanted to let you know about the story. Have a good night."

"Good night."

Javier had such mixed emotions. He was extremely excited that Chevita had called to let him know that his interview was finally going to air. This was great news, and he hoped it would bring awareness to the situation in Cuba. On the other hand he could tell that Chevita was still extremely upset with him about their conversation on Thanksgiving night. He did not know if this story was the end of any communication they would have, or if he could redeem himself. Either way he knew he had some work to do to win her over again.

On December 29th, Javier's interview finally aired. Although it was a good interview, it was not as revolutionary as Chevita and Javier had hoped, but it was also not as destructive as Nick had feared. Typical viewing audiences tuned in that night, so millions of Americans were now aware of the story in Cuba. After the story aired it appeared as though life went on as usual. There was not any public outrage at NNC for airing a story about Cuba in the midst of the stories about terrorism. There also was not any public outrage for the struggle in Cuba. The good news was that the story had now been heard, and hopefully the right people had watched.

The next morning when Chevita arrived to work she had a beautiful bouquet of flowers waiting for her with a note, "Thanks for everything. I think we make a great team. I know you are not happy with me, but after this is all over I hope you can give me a second chance. Love, Javier." Chevita sat there for a minute thinking of whether or not she wanted to give Javier a second chance, and what that even meant since they were never truly a couple. Why did guys never seem to care about women until after they realized they screwed up?

Chevita decided her office was not the place to be thinking about her love life or lack thereof. She moved the flowers to her window sill. When she returned to her desk she read a second note that must have been under her flowers, "Come see me in my office, John Wilson." Chevita could feel her heart pounding. Was she being fired? If Nick wanted to get rid of her, why could he not be a man and do it himself? If she was not being fired why would the CEO of NNC want to meet with his new field reporter, the very next morning after her interview with Javier? Even worse if she was fired, how would the plot of Vice President Gamble and General Wallace be exposed?

CEO Wilson had the corner office in one of the nicest office buildings in Washington DC. Even though the building was only eight stories tall, it felt like it might as well have been eighty stories to Chevita as she took the elevator to the top floor. Chevita was nearly sick with stress as the CEO's assistant escorted her to his office.

"Chevita, good to see you, please close the door," John Wilson sounded calm but direct.

"Good to see you too, what would you like to discuss?"

"We have not spoken much since you started, but I heard from Nick that you were doing great work."

"Thank you, Mr. Wilson."

"Please call me John. Anyway most people do not realize this, but did you know I actually graduated from West Point in 1990 before spending four years in the Army?"

"I did not, that is very admirable of you." Chevita was wondering where this was going.

"Well when I was at West Point, one of my classmates named Derrick was always whining about how hard school was, and saying how he could not wait to be an officer so he would finally be in charge. Anyway I could not stand Derrick, but I never let him know that. Do you know what Derrick is up to these days?"

"No Sir, it does not sound like he would make a very good officer if he was always whining, so I doubt he is still in the military."

"Well he must have changed his ways, because now he is a General and in charge of all military forces in Cuba."

"Oh, you are talking about General Wallace?"

"You know him?"

"Let's just say I did my homework."

"Although I never really cared for him much, we still share the West Point connection, so General Wallace called me last night. Let's just say he was not very happy."

Chevita already knew why but she played it off well, "Why was that sir."

"He saw your interview with Javier Hernandez, and he did not like the way our military was portrayed in Cuba. I told him I would talk to you and work it all out. He requested a rebuttal interview, so you are going to interview General Wallace on January 5th. Is that clear?"

"Absolutely, thank you sir."

"Just for the record I really enjoyed your story. Good job."

"Thank you."

Chevita left John Wilson's office with the completely opposite emotion she entered his office. She was ecstatic. Not only was she not being fired, but the CEO was happy with her story. Even better General Wallace played right into her plan. She thought she might have to fight to get an interview with the General, but he had now requested an interview. Chevita felt like she was back in the driver's seat. She wanted to share her great news with someone, so she decided to put the past behind her and call Javier.

"Hello,"

"Chevita! So good to hear from you. I guess you received your flowers?"

"I did, but this has nothing to do with the flowers, thanks though."

Javier was a little dismayed at how quickly she blew off his gesture, "Oh, Ok, what's up then?"

"Guess who I have an interview with on January 5th?"

"Who?"

"General Wallace, he saw your interview, and he was so infuriated that he called my CEO to request a rebuttal interview."

"Oh wow, it sounds like your plan is all coming together."

"Our plan," Chevita threw out as a peace offering.

"You did all the work"

"I could have never gotten this far without you, thank you!"

"You're welcome, I 'm just glad it is all coming together. Keep it going!"

"And just so you know I'm still mad at you, but the flowers were a good step in the right direction."

"I'm glad you liked them."

"Good night Javier."

"Good night."

Chapter 20

The morning after she learned of her interview with General Wallace, Chevita called Bo Vance to discuss the plan with him. She really needed Bo to be involved in the interview, since he would play an important part in providing a credible conflicting point of view with General Wallace. Chevita knew that Bo would be jeopardizing his future in the military if their plan did not go as expected, but she was hoping he was willing to take that risk. The biggest trick would be to get Bo invited to the interview with General Wallace. Chevita also had a plan for that.

"Hey Bo, it's Chevita."

"How are you?"

"Doing great, I have big news. General Wallace saw the interview with Javier, and he did not like the way the US military was portrayed, so he requested a rebuttal interview on January 5th."

"So what is your plan for the interview? Do you plan to expose the conversations with the Vice President we discussed on militant rule in the United States? Or just focus on Cuba?"

"I would really like to just focus on the troops being in Cuba, and why they are still there. I want to address the issue of possible militant rule in the United States with

Vice President Gamble, and I want to catch him off guard with the topic. In regard to the interview with General Wallace I could really use your help. I need you to find a way to be invited to the interview."

"Why do I need to be there?"

"I need you to give your expert opinion on the United States military presence in Cuba."

"But it will be in conflict with General Wallace. That puts me in an extremely difficult position."

"I realize that, but if all goes as planned with the General Wallace interview and the Vice President Gamble interview, then he will not remain a General much longer."

"But what if it doesn't?"

"We cannot fail. Right now Vice President Gamble is a clear front runner to be the next President. He has everything that the American public is looking for: charisma, class, respect, and a beautiful family. He will be elected if we fail to expose his plan, and if what you tell me is true about the talks between he and General Wallace then life as we know it will forever be changed."

"Ok, I'm in, so what do we do now."

"From what you tell me, it sounds like General Wallace really leans on you to handle the operations in

Cuba. We need him to think he should also lean on you for this interview. Tomorrow is the New Year holiday, but on January 2nd, go visit General Wallace. Bring up how outraged you were at the Javier interview, and ask if he saw it. Inevitably he will bring up the interview he has with me on the 5th, and at that point ask if he would like you to join him. Tell him that by presenting a cohesive front the two of you will be able to make a more convincing argument on why it is important for the United States military to stay in Cuba."

"So you want me to lie to the General?"

"I don't care what you have to do, but I need you in that interview."

"I will do everything I can to make it happen."

"Thanks, let me know what you find out."

"I will."

The next couple of days seemed like an eternity to Chevita. She worked through New Year's Eve and New Year's Day digging up every fact she could on Cuba and General Wallace. Even though she was extremely busy, she could not stop thinking about how she could handle the interview if Bo did not participate. She knew if she did not have a credible conflicting point of view with the General then the interview would come across as just her vs General Wallace. If that were the case she did not stand a chance as she was a new face to the nation, and her credibility did not hold a candle to that of the General. January 2nd came and went and she still had not heard back from Bo. She was relieved the next day when she received a call.

"Chevita, it's Bo," he already sounded defeated.

"Hey Bo, is everything ok?"

"I'm afraid I let you down, I talked to the General, and he told me he was flying to DC on the 4th, and to 'hold the fort down' but he would not even tell me why he was going. I think he might be suspicious of me."

"Ahhh, well thanks for trying, I hope I can pull this off."

Immediately Bo's tone changed, "I'm just screwing with you, my flight is all booked, I will be in DC tomorrow."

"You're an ass, but that really had me going. If this military thing does not work out I will introduce you to some TV exec's. You could have a future in acting. I'm so happy to hear you are going to be a part of this interview. What is your flight information? I would like to meet you and General Wallace at the airport. Also dinner is on me tomorrow night at the finest steakhouse in Georgetown."

"We are on DL76 arriving into Dulles at 1530. See you tomorrow. I'm looking forward to a quality steak dinner. I've been eating rice and beans for far too long."

"See you tomorrow, have a safe flight."

The next day Chevita met Bo and and General Wallace at Dulles International Airport promptly at 3:30 PM. She was extremely professional, and handed each of them sample interview questions. General Wallace was pleased to accept her offer for a steak dinner. Chevita and Bo had hoped for a nice relaxing dinner for the three of them to get acquainted so that everyone would be more at ease going into the interview. Everything went exactly as planned, by his third glass of scotch the General was having a great time. Chevita actually enjoyed the company of Bo and General Wallace. She had villianized him for so long that she was surprised at how much she liked the General as a person. By the end of dinner she was referring to him as Derrick, and no longer General Wallace. She had to convince herself to really stick to her guns when it came to the interview, because of how much was on the line.

The vibe was entirely different the next day when Bo and General Wallace entered the studio for their live interview. The General was all business and though they all had a good time the night before, today Chevita was clearly the enemy in his eyes. Chevita started the interview by introducing Bo and General Wallace, followed by small talk on their experiences. She spent a good amount of time establishing Bo as a credible source including his education at West Point, and his experience in Cuba. Chevita tried to paint a picture of Bo as the true leader in Cuba, and General Wallace more as a figure head sitting in his office smoking cigars. The plan appeared to be working, and it was clear to anyone watching that the General's blood was beginning to boil. It was then that Chevita posed the question that she knew would send him over the edge.

"I want to address this question to both of you, as I am interested to hear what each of you has to say from each of your perspectives as the top two US military officers in Cuba. After nearly seven years of running what appears to be a militant rule in Cuba, do you think it is time for the United States to remove their troops, and allow Cuba to become an independent nation?"

"I'll take this one Bo," the General quickly responded.

Chevita cut him off before he could proceed, "No, I would like if each of you could answer the question, as you could have different perspectives. I am sure the American public would love to hear from both of you. Bo I would prefer for you to respond to the question first, as I would like to conclude the interview with General Wallace's closing thoughts." General Wallace turned bright red with anger at this point.

Before he answered Bo looked over to the General and then back to Chevita with a nervous yet determined look on his face, "The US military occupation in Cuba is not working. There are people all over the island protesting for what they believed was promised to them after the revolution ended in 2019, that Cuba would become a free and independent nation. I have witnessed firsthand these protests turn more and more violent. Why is the United States even still in Cuba? We have never gotten a straight answer. I believe with the current state of events in the world that our troops could be better used elsewhere to protect the United States from terrorism."

At this point General Wallace had enough. He stood up and put his finger is Bo's face, "What the hell is wrong with you. You are going to be directly insubordinate to your superior officer on national television. I hope you know your military career is over." General Wallace then turned to Chevita, "I'll have you know that your CEO John Wilson was a West Point classmate of mine, and I will be sure that he is made fully aware of what happened here today. I know that you and this piece-of-shit conspired against me. I did not become a General by being a dumbass, and although you are not in the military you have underestimated my power. You better start looking for a new job, because you will be fired."

The interview ended with General Wallace storming out of the studio, and Chevita making her closing statement. The interview made for excellent television, and it propelled Chevita, Bo Vance, and General Wallace to household names. After the bombing in Detroit the average American supported the views of Bo Vance, and agreed with his questioning of why the United States military was still in Cuba. Bo never actually defied or undermined General Wallace. He simply answered the question Chevita presented first, so there was nothing he could truly be punished for. Chevita's job was also safe as she had the highest ratings of any news reporter in the country that week. John Wilson was a business man first, and he would not ruin a good thing with one of his top reporters for a classmate from over thirty years ago that he did not even care for. Step two of their plan was a success, and the stage was set beautifully for Chevita's interview with Vice President Gamble in four days with the entire nation tuning in.

Chapter 21

Following the interview with Bo Vance and General Wallace, Chevita was happier than she had been since she moved to Washington DC. The plan she developed with Javier and Bo was all coming together, but with the interview with Vice President Gamble coming up she could not lose focus. Chevita spent the next three days researching everything she could find on the Vice President, and developing a line of questioning for the interview that would hopefully result in exposing his true motives should he win the 2026 Presidential election. Going into January 2026 Vice President Gamble held a commanding lead in all of the polls by a margin of 66% to Senator Franklin's 34%. He had the Presidential image and charisma that the American public was looking for. He was very well spoken, but he always managed to dodge the truly important Presidential issues in favor of speaking about hot topic social issues of the day. Chevita wanted to be the first to change that in her interview with the Vice President. Hot off of a great interview with General Wallace, an estimated 70 million Americans tuned in to watch Chevita interview Vice President Gamble on January 9, 2026.

"Thank you for joining me Mr. Vice President."

"Thank you for having me, I've been looking forward to this interview for quite some time."

"I want to start by congratulating you on taking such a resounding lead in the polls, this is likely the greatest margin held by a candidate at this point of a campaign since Ronald Reagan in the 1980s."

"I appreciate the comparison to such a great President, but we have not won anything at this point. We have a long way to go, but I am pleased that the American public is taking notice of what we stand for."

"That is exactly what I hope to address with you here today. What is it that you stand for, and more specifically if elected what sort of policies could we expect from the White House?"

"I'm glad you asked. I stand for a safer and more secure America, one that will be free from the horrific terrorist events that took place in Detroit just six weeks ago."

"I think we can all agree that we would like to be safe, but we should dive more into the specifics Americans can expect from you should you be elected."

"Sure, I am an open book, what would you like to hear."

"Were you able to see the interview I conducted with the Commander of Military Operations in Cuba,

General Wallace, and his second in charge Bo Vance a few days ago?"

"I caught a couple of headlines, but I did not see the interview first hand. You know the campaign trail can be very busy."

"Yes I understand, well let's just say that General Wallace and Bo Vance did not see eye to eye on the American military's involvement in Cuba. Bo was asked the question, 'After nearly seven years of running what appears to be a militant rule in Cuba, do you think it is time for the United States to remove their troops, and allow Cuba to become an independent nation,' to which he responded, 'The US military occupation in Cuba is not working. There are people all over the island protesting for what they believed was promised to them after the revolution ended in 2019, that Cuba would become a free and independent nation. I have witnessed firsthand these protests turn more and more violent. Why is the United States even still in Cuba, we have never gotten a straight answer? I believe with the current state of events in the World that our troops could be better used elsewhere to protect the United States from terrorism.' If elected, how do you plan to address the presence of the US military in Cuba?"

"I would like to start by saying our military men and women have my full-fledged support and respect. One thing I will agree with in Bo Vance's response is that we do need to protect the United States from terrorism. I think as a nation that should be our focus."

"Protecting the United States from terrorism is important, and we will get to that, but what about the question at hand. If elected how do you plan to address the presence of the US military in Cuba?"

"Although I respect Bo Vance and what he does with on a daily basis for our country I disagree that the method of government in Cuba is not working. General Wallace is doing a fine job turning that island around. In fact if elected I plan to appoint General Wallace as the official head of Government in Cuba. The World is a dangerous place, and who better to maintain a safe society than the United States military."

"That makes it sound as if you believe a militant rule would be the best form of government in the United States as well."

"It sounds like you are taking words out of my mouth. I did not say that militant rule would be the best form of government in the United States. I simply said that the world is a dangerous place, and that the people of Cuba could feel safe in the hands of the US military."

"Do you not believe that the citizens of Cuba deserve the opportunity to establish their own independent government as they have expressed their desire to do so, modeled on the government of the United States that has been successful for 250 years?"

"I do not believe that model of government would work everywhere, and that it is actually an archaic form of limited government. The people in any country ours included would be better off with a stronger government that would protect the people."

"What do you mean by stronger government? Are you now suggesting a militant rule in the United States?"

"Militant rule has such a negative connotation. I would call it a stronger government with a central leader that could make quick decisions to protect the people, similar to the government that would be established under General Wallace in Cuba."

"But don't you realize the negative impact that could have. You would be taking out the checks and balances system of both Houses of Congress and the Supreme Court."

"No, the United States will always maintain both Houses of Congress and the Supreme Court, they would just serve more as advisors on how laws should be made and what laws should stand up. The President would do the same job he does now, but he would just have slightly more power. The process simply takes too long in modern times when governments need to be able to rapidly respond to changing events. It is unacceptable that we have not had any direct action on the bombing in Detroit that happened nearly 6 weeks ago. Under my plan government action would have been taken the next day through an executive order. Congress takes entirely too long to reach a consensus. I can be that consensus immediately, and we can see the change that America needs immediately."

"But you would be undermining freedom in the United States, and the structure of government that has been in place for 250 years. What you are saying would have much further consequences than just responding to one bombing, you would basically be acting as a totalitarian dictator."

"Once again that has such a negative connotation. I would prefer the position to keep the title of President."

"Call it what you will, but I think we all know that what you are suggesting if elected is a dictatorship."

"Dictators take over through force. I am running for President in a free and open election in the greatest country ever created. I would serve the standard term, and if reelected serve a total of 8 years. I do not intend on becoming a dictator. I only want to protect the country that I love, and I think the best way to do that is to give the President more power."

"I do not think the American public realized what you stood for until today, thank you for sharing with the nation your political views and policies."

"Did you not want to discuss any issues other than Cuba?"

"I think you said it all, thank you for your time, and I wish you the best moving forward."

Vice President Gamble's political views had finally been brought to light. The polls that came out on January 13th had completely reversed. It did not matter what Senator Franklin said in his January 11th interview, the voters knew he was a better choice for President than Vice President Gamble. Senator Franklin now held a commanding lead over Vice President Gamble, so much so that the Vice President removed himself from the race. Chevita had very likely changed the course of history, and possibly prevented a great deal of bloodshed on American soil. Senator Franklin was not a perfect candidate, but he was also not going to destroy the country in one election. Unless someone else entered the race and made a statement in a hurry Senator Franklin was a sure bet to win the 2026 election, thanks to Chevita.

Chapter 22

Although she was not aware President Thomas Morgan was a big fan of Chevita. In fact he had watched Javier's interview, General Wallace and Bo Vance's interview, and Vice President Morgan's interview. It was clear to anyone who had watched all three interviews that the United States military should be removed from Cuba. The poll that came out on January 13th showed that an overwhelming 85% of American's believed that the US military should remove the troops from Cuba, and that Cuba should be granted independence. Before watching Chevita's interviews and seeing the response of the American public, President Morgan had intended on gliding into retirement after his last year in office. He knew that was no longer going to be an option, and on January 14th President Morgan decided that now was the time to act. Unlike Vice President Gamble, President Morgan respected the Constitution of the United States so he went before Congress to plead his case that the US military should be removed from Cuba, and they should be granted independence. Both the House and the Senate voted the next day in favor of President Morgan's case.

On January 19th, 2026 President Morgan traveled to Havana to meet with Javier and Governor Puig to sign an agreement to remove all troops and grant Cuban independence. Chevita was on hand to report the story, and Bo Vance was also there as a good will ambassador. The public perception of Bo Vance had changed in Cuba after his interview with Chevita. That afternoon President Morgan addressed a crowd of 200,000 in Plaza Vieja.

"It is fitting that on Martin Luther King Jr Day we sign this agreement in recognition of Cuban independence. Javier Hernandez has followed the example set by Dr. King by leading a series of non-violent protests to fight for civil liberties. Today, Javier along with the rest of Cuba realizes their dream of living in a free nation. We hope that today is the start of new mutually beneficial partnership between the United States and the independent nation of Cuba. The United States would like to see our neighbors to the south prosper, and we are willing to provide any counsel necessary to help this wonderful country establish a democratic government. With the signing of this agreement, the United States has agreed to remove all troops from Cuba by February 1st. Governor Puig would you like to address the citizens of Cuba?" At this point the crowd erupted, Cuban flags were waving, and fireworks were going off towards the back of the crowd.

"Thank you Mr. President. We truly appreciate your kind words and your presence with us here today. I would like to clarify a few things for our citizens. First of all I have no intention of reestablishing a dictatorship in Cuba. I plan to step down as governor effective May 1st, and remove the position entirely. President Morgan and I have made arrangements to establish an American Embassy in Havana. I will work with advisors from the United States at the embassy to establish a new government structure. The general plan for our new government will be based upon the checks and balances system established in the United States 250 years ago. Our government like that of the United States will be comprised of a legislative branch to make laws, a judicial branch to ensure the laws are just, and an executive branch to carry out laws and lead Cuba. The rest of the details will be developed over the next month with counsel from the United States. Our first election as an independent nation has been a long time coming, so we plan to expedite the process. On March 20th I will release all of the details on how our country will be divided into districts. Once the districts are established any Cuban citizen over the age of 18 will have the ability to nominate a representative for congress and a candidate for President by March 30th. The top three individuals with the most nominations in each district will then be on the election ballot on May 1st. That is enough of me boring you about politics. Although I have been governor for the past seven years, Javier Hernandez has been your true leader. Javier would you like to address your people?"

"Pres-I-Den-Te (clap, clap, clapclapclap) Pres-I-Den-Te" before Javier could even say a word the crowd of 200,000 erupted in a chant.

"CUBA, I LOVE YOU! Thank you, Thank you, I am humbled. We as Cubans should be proud of how far we have come, but I want us to focus on our future to prevent making the mistakes of our past. For the first time in your life the future of Cuba is in your hands, get out and vote on May 1st. While I have this stage I would like to give a special thank you to two people whom without them this day may have never come. Bo Vance, thank you, we did not always see eye to eye, but you definitely came through for Cuba and stood up for freedom when it mattered most. Thank you for putting your neck on the line, I know it was not easy. Chevita Diaz, could you come join me on stage?"

Chevita instantly felt her stomach drop, even though she reported the news to millions of viewers each night, she had never been in front of a crowd of 200,000 with all eyes on her. Chevita always had a hard time telling Javier no, so even with her extreme case of nervousness Chevita made her way to the stage.

"I want you all to meet someone very special to me. There is no way any of us would be here right now if it was not for this woman. She was born in 1995 in Miami to Cuban parents who defected in the 1980s. Although she was born American her Cuban blood runs through her veins. That Cuban blood inspired her to lead a revolution for Cuba. It may not have been a revolution in the sense that we think of a revolution, but the crusade that Chevita led through the news was a carefully planned revolution that led to our freedom. If you look back over the past few weeks to her interview of me, her interview of General Wallace and our friend Bo Vance, and to her interview of Vice President Gamble, I am sure you will agree. She is absolutely brilliant, and damn isn't she gorgeous. Chevita I am madly in love with you, and nothing would make me happier than for you to say yes to the question I plan to ask you right here in front of the 200,000 people I love most in the World. Chevita will you marry me?"

Chevita was trembling with shock, she had known since day one that she loved Javier, the timing just never was quite right, until now. Chevita was at a loss for words, "Yes, Yes, I will."

The crowd erupted; it was a story book ending to the day Javier and Chevita had long dreamed of. Of course Chevita and Javier would have much to discuss in regard to their future, but for now all that mattered was that they would have a future together.

Epilogue

The next few months were a whirlwind for Javier and Chevita. Javier and Orlando agreed to travel to the United States for the first time with Chevita. They took the new high speed ferry from Havana to Miami to visit Chevita's parents where she was excited to introduce them to Javier, and tell them the news. She was surprised when she found out that her father already knew. Javier had done his research to contact Professor Diaz from the University of Miami to ask for his daughter's hand.

After spending a week with her parents Chevita, Javier, and Orlando traveled to DC where she continued her job as usual for three weeks until Javier received a call on March 30th to let him know he had the most nominations for President of anyone in Cuba. The people of Cuba already knew what Javier stood for, so he decided he would forego campaigning and would not run any slanderous ads against his competitors. Javier was hoping by staying out of the spotlight during the election season that he would set a precedent that future elections would be based upon optimism, and not just putting down your political opponent.

After hearing that Javier was on the ballot, Chevita knew he would be elected. On April 1st, 2026 Chevita put her two weeks' notice in at NNC and moved to Havana with Javier. Chevita left on good terms with her executive producer, and with the CEO of NNC. She was assured that she would always have a job available should she ever decide to return to DC.

Javier was elected as the first President of the new Cuban Government, and Chevita became the first lady when they married two months later. Javier was able to lead Cuba for the first eight years under the new government, and in her typical fashion, Chevita set the bar high for future first ladies in Cuba. Through the support of Javier, she led sweeping reforms to provide Cubans a higher quality of life. Neither of them ever dreamed their life would turn out the way it did, but they proved with hard work and a little faith that they could change the world.

Made in the USA
Charleston, SC
04 May 2015